D1479268

THE
GENE
SOLUTION

MIKE ROCHELLE

The Gene Solution

Copyright © 2021 by Michael Rochelle Jr.

Print ISBN: 978-1-09838-3-343

eBook ISBN: 978-1-09838-3-350

TO THE REALISTS;

YOU CAN MAKE IT REAL.

O.

IT WAS ONE OF THOSE APRIL DAYS WHERE
you felt the seasons were at war with each other. Winter was not going
to cede to Spring on this clear but frigid Saturday. The ground was
covered in frost, almost like the Earth wanted to prevent the shovels
from digging the six feet necessary to bury the dead. The only sound
was the crunch of dress shoes as a small gathering followed a simple
brown casket up a small rise.

The Galloway family hadn't expected to bury their son, Henry, at
Woodland cemetery. It was their older son, Tripp, who had suggested
it. The Wright Brothers were buried there and Henry always dreamt
of becoming a pilot in between hospital visits and trying to breathe.
It was the least the family could do: bury their son in a place that
seemed fitting.

With the final crunch of shoes, and the last piece of dirt moved,
the ceremony began. The casket was placed next to the hole in the cus-
tomary way. Everyone kept staring at the casket, willing its passenger
to get up. Seventeen years old was too young for someone to pass away.
It's like one firework, and then nothing.

No one mentioned it at the funeral, but Henry was dealt a shit hand. They mentioned his kindness, or bravery but never his terrible luck. It was plain and simple; he lost the genetic roll of the dice and ended up with cystic fibrosis. The random combination of Mom and Dad's DNA brought forth a baby boy who fell on the wrong side of 25 percent and, with that, a lifetime of struggle. The Galloways were a simple family who wanted to have a simple life. Fate decided that wasn't going to be the case.

Standing next to his casket was Henry's brother, Tripp. In a rumpled suit and close-cropped hair, he hugged his mother as a silent tear rolled down his face. Flying home from Massachusetts as soon as he heard Henry had pneumonia, Tripp barely had time to say goodbye. Henry, his Hal Pal, that's what Tripp called him anyways, was gone. As the casket was lowered into the damned hole in the ground, Tripp released his mother, picked up some dirt and tossed it in. He looked down at the casket and knew that it could have been him. His time in medical school, if it only taught him one thing, is that it could have been him. It should have been him, he thought. Hal was a better human overall. Silently crying, the gathering made their way back to the cars. With the opening and slamming of doors piercing the quiet, Tripp looked back at that little rise. It was the 25 percent that was bothering him. Why did his brother have to be the 25 percent?

I.

APPROVED.

That was the gist of the email that Dr. Allen Charles 'Tripp' Galloway had just read to himself six times. Falling back into his office chair, slumped and numb, he couldn't believe it. After all these years, he had finally done it.

Tripp convinced the Food and Drug Administration (FDA) to start an international, multi-center, double-blind, Phase III clinical trial that would end sickle cell anemia. What that actually meant is that Tripp was going to wipe that shit stain of a disease off the face of the planet and the FDA was going to let him. The FDA, the goalkeeper to his dream, just let him score.

Tripp wasn't some head in the clouds, "save the hippos," type of doctor. He was a realist. It's what kept his patients from believing that he can do it all. At this moment, Tripp himself was beyond surprised. He had truly outdone himself. The FDA is the arbiter of risk when it comes to clinical life in the United States. This approval was a vote of confidence in the doctor.

Tripp reached under his desk to the mini-fridge. It was the one thing in his practice that wasn't ornate. Simple, black and filled with Coca-Cola, it fit directly under his desk. The man, although generally healthy, had an immense caffeine addiction.

Next to the stacks of soda was one bottle of Chandon. Taped to the bottle was a bright pink note that stated, "Fuck you sickle cell ... Love, The Team."

Getting excited, Tripp ripped coffee mugs and glasses off the shelf and hurriedly walked into the hallway. If you followed the light blue walls to the right, they would come to clinical grade labs with incubators, water baths, centrifuges and microscopes, gleaming in the artificial light.

A little further, there were rooms to see patients. Tripp hated those rooms. As an OB/GYN and fertility specialist, he always delivered news in those rooms. Parents found out if they could ever raise a child of their own ... ever. It really was a crap shoot depending on the day. He told Aiden, his assistant and trial manager, to schedule patients so that it was a healthy mix of shitty and great news. Some days it was rough. Telling three couples in a row they couldn't have children was never a great time. Finally, at the end of the hall is the waiting room. It was filled with brown leather chairs, a flat screen television and the latest news about the Genetic superstars – Galloway and Stein, Tripp's private practice.

Tripp turned left and opened the door into the break room. Tony, Tara, Michelle and Aiden were gathered around the table eating the meal of the day. It looked like tacos. Tony Kim, a self-described "bad Korean" had three-quarters of a taco in his mouth when he looked up.

"Doc, what's up? You want some?" Tony asked with guacamole on his face.

Tony, a short stocky guy with a buzzed head and tattoos, oftentimes forgot his manners. Tripp didn't mind, though, because Tony was a magician when it came to culturing cells. Without Tony, the business would fail.

"No, where's Morti?" Tripp asked quickly.

Tara and Michelle were eyeing the champagne. You would think those girls were boozehounds instead of nurses. Aiden, knowing damn well what that bottle meant, stood quickly and said over his shoulder, "His wife called; I'll get him."

Tara and Michelle continued to eye the champagne as they pounded down tacos. Nothing got in the way of their food. Tara and Michelle looked like twins except one was from New Jersey and the other was from Vermont. With her curiosity sufficiently riled, Tara managed to squeeze out a "What's the occasion Doc?" as she polished off her fourth taco.

Tripp ignored the question as Aiden and Morti strode in. Dr. Mortimer Stein was the opposite of Tripp in most ways. While Tripp was tall, white and horribly single, Morti was short, black and horribly married.

It all started when Tripp met Morti at Harvard Medical School. Morti was attending a lecture on Epigenetics when Tripp plopped himself down next to him. Epigenetics, or the study of how the environment can alter your genetic expression, is a little dry. Morti and Tripp commiserated on how boring the talk was and it was history from there. The two things that bothered Tripp was that Morti was a Red Sox fan (Fuck the Sox) and Morti had gotten into Tripp's dream school, Boston University. So naturally, fuck BU Med. What Tripp liked the most about Morti was that he had a sense of humor. Morti would often use his name and appearance to his advantage. Most people don't expect a Mortimer Stein to appear as Morti does. Mortimer Stein was adopted by an infertile Jewish couple living on the lower east side, not too far away from their now lower west side office.

Morti, spotting the bottle, looked up. "What's with the 'Fuck you bottle'?"

Galloway couldn't control himself, with a grin he said, "They fucking approved it. We did it!"

Michelle, still chugging along on her tacos said, "*Madre de Dios*, you're kidding me right? The FDA is gonna let us do that shit?"

"Are we getting raises?" Tara asked.

Aiden was silently beaming and Tony let out an "Oh Shit". They fucking did it.

The bottle was popped, champagne was poured and appointments were canceled for the day. Tara and Michelle pulled out a bottle of Smirnoff from some mysterious filing cabinet. Aiden ordered enough dumplings from his favorite place on Mott to feed a small army.

As the festivities continued, Tripp raised a small test tube of Smirnoff and looked at the team. "You all have worked so hard to get to this point and Morti and I can't thank you enough. With a little luck, we're gonna be the people who make sickle cell a thing of the past. So with that, fuck you sickle cell. Cheers!"

Hours, and about seven shots later, Tripp was dropped off by an Uber in front of his Upper West Side brownstone. A simple oak door stood in between Tripp and another drink. The hangover was going to be unholy, but he didn't care. It was a celebratory hangover. It also meant that he would be going to Jacob's Pickles tomorrow morning. A co-op platter was calling his name.

Tripp unlocked the front door and immediately went to the bar cart. While making a vodka and ginger ale, he clicked on the stereo and took a seat. It was nearly an impossible feat, getting the wimpy fuck Myers to approve the trial. That FDA schmuck really had no balls. He understood the hesitation though. An infertility specialist and a geneticist wanted to eliminate the sickle cell mutation from the human race. The trial would take years, if not a decade. The money it would take: astronomical. The process was pretty simple, but in thousands of people it would take time.

The trial itself was a technical wonder, thanks to Aiden. An international, multi-center, double-blind, Phase III clinical trial was serious business. Each word is packed with nuance and added difficulty. International: they were looking at patients from all over the world. Multi-center: they were collecting samples from multiple locations. Double-blind: Nobody knew which patients received the treatment or a placebo. Phase III: It was to be conducted on humans.

The affected patients would come into clinics around the world and give their bone marrow. The bone marrow would be sent to Aiden and randomly selected to be treated or be a placebo. If the marrow is chosen to be a placebo, that sucks for them. All they get back is their marrow and their sickle cell. However, the marrow that is chosen for the procedure is sent to Tony and Stein. They create stem cells and, using the CRISPR/ Cas-9 editing platform, edit the affected patients' DNA. Voila, no more sickle cell. This means eighty thousand Americans and millions of other people would be able to live happy and healthy lives.

This CRISPR/Cas-9 platform utilizes nature to cut out the nucleotides, or DNA building blocks, and replace them with whatever you want. The Cas-9 does the cutting while the CRISPR does the switching.

Tripp had to admit, nature was brilliant sometimes. From there, and this is the cool part, surgeons conduct full bone marrow transfusions, thereby eliminating any sickle cell anemia in the previously affected patient.

Of course, the process of complete cell switch over took some time. Also, women's eggs were never switched as women are born with all of their eggs. They might have a problem if they decide to have children. It didn't matter though, within three generations the mutation would be gone except for reversions, or random mutations that turned sickle cell back on. This is due to the way sickle cell is inherited in people, both parents need to pass on the gene to their child, falling on the wrong side of 25 percent. By changing the males, that cannot happen.

Tripp was pleased. After fifteen years of school and hard-work, he finally, at age thirty-five, was the man he thought he should be. His mother would disagree, but honestly, he didn't give a shit; he was single and successful, not married and miserable. He could do what and whom he wanted.

This was just the beginning too. In a couple of years, if all went to plan, they'd be putting him in the history books. As he tipped his glass back and headed to his bed, Tripp thought of all the work that was to come, hopefully with a decent helping of fame.

II.

EIGHT YEARS AND TWO WEEKS LATER.

17 OCTOBER 2025

NEW YORK, NEW YORK

"GOOD MORNING, I'M LEE GOLDBERG AND today is a day that will go down in history as a team of researchers on the lower west side just announced that they have found a cure for sickle cell anemia. We have with us now, Dr. Allen Galloway, one of the doctors responsible for the discovery. Thank you Dr. Galloway for joining us this morning."

In a navy blue pinstripe suit, Tripp was basking in his new fame. He had barely finished his coffee and crossword puzzle when Aiden had called him. They had wanted either Morti or Tripp on *The Today Show* in two hours. Aiden had released the statement yesterday about the cure and the phones hadn't stopped ringing since.

"Good Morning Lee, and please, call me Tripp."

"Alright Tripp, so sickle cell anemia is a genetic disease right? You can't catch it."

Trip was prepped fifteen minutes before the interview and knew how the questions were supposed to go.

"That's right Lee, so when a child is born, they are made up of both their parents. The father donates 50 percent of his DNA while the mother contributes the other half. Oftentimes, a certain combination of genes can lead to disease. This is the case with sickle cell. Both your father and mother donate the sickle cell gene. When that happens a baby is born with the sickle cell."

"So how do you, and Dr. Stein, cure the disease?"

Tripp was glad they had mentioned Dr. Stein. His team would have killed him if he didn't mention them. "Dr. Stein, myself, and the rest of our team, really work together to treat every patient. Without Michelle, Tara, Aiden and Tony, Dr. Stein and I would be lost. But, to answer your question, what we do is take the patient's bone marrow and edit the DNA. We then replace their bone marrow with the newly edited sample. So we end up replacing all of their marrow with their new and healthy stuff."

"That's absolutely incredible. It's safe?"

"Absolutely. We plan to eradicate sickle cell from the United States within two years. We hope to do this to children when they are born. The children will not have to suffer the consequences," Tripp said deftly. He really liked giving interviews. The lights and cameras were amazing. It also helped that the staff was mostly cute women. Tripp had to remind himself to buy Aiden a Venti Caramel Macchiato later. He would definitely want to keep him on his good side with all the interview opportunities coming up.

Tripp almost forgot that Lee was there while daydreaming. He snapped back to reality at the second half of the question.

" … and so do you think we could possibly do this before people are born?"

Tripp was not ready for that question. Fumbling to answer, he had to come up with something. "I assume that would be reasonable. As an infertility specialist myself and Dr. Stein as a geneticist, it would make sense to modify the egg and sperm in order to allow for normal development of the child. Dr. Stein and I partnered together due to his abilities and the unique resources I have due to my specialty. With that logic, though, it could be the possible next step. I wouldn't want to do anything when the baby is in-utero. In my opinion, that would be too high risk to both the child developing in the womb and the mother carrying the child."

Tripp had broken a slight sweat. He could feel it collecting on his back. He hoped he answered the question well enough. As Lee continued to lob questions, Tripp couldn't stop wondering how he never thought of going to the embryo before? *Partially because the FDA would probably never approve it,* Tripp thought. *Playing God was not part of the FDA credo even though that fuck Myers believes he has the right to. Ever since that one screw up with the blood tube, he has been riding our trial like a fly rides shit. One person dies and all of a sudden the trial isn't worth it. What an asshole. But what if we could get the FDA to go for it though? It could be worth a shot. I'd have to talk to Morti about it.*

"And now my final question Tripp, you and Dr. Stein have garnered some serious attention since your announcement yesterday. People are calling you Ebony and Ivory, Dr. Perfect and Dr. Love, the best pair to come to medicine and visionaries. How does all that sound?"

"I think the real question is am I Dr. Perfect or Dr. Love?" Tripp said jokingly.

As the camera veered away and Lee Goldberg sent the feed down to Al Roker, Tripp gave out a sigh of relief. It was a good first interview. The bigger question now, thanks to Lee Goldberg, was what's next?

TURKISH CONSULATE

LONDON, UNITED KINGDOM

Slavomir Krukov was bored. His wife Anna made him come to these types of things, but honestly, he didn't give a shit about any of the fucks he was pretending to engage with. They were weak and foul specimens of human life.

As the last rays of light were pulled down over the Turkish Consulate, the party began to take on a more rambunctious tone. Casually, sipping his neat vodka, he kept an eye on his wife and her bodyguard as they moved through the groups of scumbags and liars. God, she was a force to be reckoned with. In her backless dress, precariously ending right above her perfectly shaped rear, not many politicians could stay away for long. Her sharp features, vivacious laugh and perfectly curled hair enchanted the poor fools. The plunging neckline didn't hurt either.

He had to admit, they did make a dashing couple. Slavomir, being a former Spetsnaz (Russian special forces) operative, stood just under two meters and kept a muscular frame at ninety-five kilograms. Slavomir, or as the people at this party decided to call him, Slav, made his fortune as a shipping baron, owning the largest import/export business in the Baltic. He was a grappling partner with Putin and was in charge of shipping all of the construction materials for the Sochi Olympics, for a hefty sum of course.

Salvomir's bodyguard leaned into his ear as the Consul from Germany was regaling him with tales from Oktoberfests' past. Apparently the Turkish Consul was getting handsy with Anna.

Excusing himself politely, Slavomir slowly walked over to his wife, handing his glass to his bodyguard. The Consul had cornered her. Slavomir came up from behind the clearly drunk Consul and placed a hand around the back of the Consul's neck, as if they were old friends. The bodyguards moved behind Slavomir, blocking anyone's view.

"Mehmet, what horrible story are you telling my wife?" As he said this, Slavomir slowly applied force to the pressure point beneath the Consul's earlobe. This sent pain signals coursing throughout his entire jaw. Mehmet couldn't seem to find his words. The bodyguards, former Spetsnaz themselves, quite enjoyed the show while blocking the gesture from the rest of the party. They admired the hands-on attitude their boss took.

Seeing that this wasn't going to end well, Anna spoke up, "Mehmet was just telling me about the Doctor who might one day design the perfect children. The doctor is already approved to cure sickle cell in the United States. Isn't that interesting?"

Her tone is what loosened the grip that Slavomir had on Mehmet's neck. Anna didn't approve of the violent underpinnings that surrounded her husband's business.

"That is interesting my love, but why would he do such a thing?" Slavomir challenged. *Let's see if Mehmet deserves to live,* he thought.

Mehmet, clearly thankful for Anna's interference, said cautiously, "He is improving the lives of countless people. It also sounded to me at least that he would be able to make perfect children, not that your children wouldn't be perfect anyways."

Mehmet had begun to sweat. Clearly, this cockroach in a human's skin was a waste of energy and time. But ... and that was a large but, he had struck a note on that last sentence.

Slavomir, with his interest now piqued, gestured to one of his bodyguards, "Mehmet, you are right, it is a great service that doctor is doing. If you would do us the honor, Alex will get you a drink. Enjoy the rest of your evening."

Mehmet was dismissed.

Mehmet didn't know that in Anna's family, there lay the gene for Hemophilia. The disease is described as X-linked recessive, so a Mother can be a carrier while any male that inherits the trait will have the disease. Slavomir did not want to risk having weak sons or daughters that could give him weak grandsons. Weakness was unacceptable.

Slavomir, now turning to his wife, switched to Russian. "Are you okay? What happened? Alex can handle him if needed."

Arkady, the other gargantuan bodyguard, smirked at the thought.

Anna, catching the smirk, quickly answered. "Everything was fine. Arkady acted too quickly. The Consul was just drunk."

Slavomir trusted Arkady with his wife's life, so he sincerely doubted Arkady acted too quickly. Accepting the answer though, Slavomir told Arkady to recall Alex. The Consul was allowed to live. As they turned to face the party again, they watched the drunk diplomats pawn for attention like strippers on poles.

Slavomir, disgusted with the lack of discipline, whispered to Arkady to ready the car. He was done for the night. They circumvented the throngs of drunks and made their way to the coat check. Anna grabbed her shawl while the bodyguards and Slavomir were given back their firearms. He hated the fact that he couldn't carry the firearms in embassies. Hence, the reason his bodyguards and himself had ceramic blades strapped to various areas of their bodies. Feeling a little more secure, Slavomir and Anna slid into their armored Mercedes-Maybach S600 and sped off to the airport.

While in the car, Slavomir asked Anna what she thought of the doctor and his curing of diseases. Anna, sensing his train of thought, diplomatically said, "I think the idea is interesting. It could be useful. You?"

Slavomir knew exactly how he felt. Anna, the love of his life, could finally bless him with strong boys. The idea certainly intrigued him. "If he could help us, I would like to meet this man."

Anna placed a hand on his thigh, gave him a wink, and looked out the window as they paralleled the Thames. Slavomir, now very inclined on getting home, leaned toward the driver's seat. "Get us home quickly and I want a full report on the doctor Mehmet was talking about." With a noticeable push, the Mercedes accelerated with ease. Banishing any further thoughts from his head, Slavomir turned his attention to Anna and what was to come.

SILVER SPRING, MARYLAND

Dennis Myers, an FDA inspector, was livid. He had just turned on *The Today Show*, hoping to catch Carrie Underwood performing her new album, and what does he get instead? Allen freaking Galloway talking on the television about his trial. Dennis couldn't believe they let the trial continue after the death of that poor man in California. *Dying from blood hemolysis must have been terrible*, Myers thought. Those

Sugar Honey Ice Tea heads in New York got away with it because of a technicality. It was a "labeling mistake," they said. "It will never happen again," they said.

Dennis was determined to halt the trial right there and somehow, Galloway convinced his bosses that he should keep going. And now, they let a potentially dangerous method onto the market. Galloway wanted to do this to seventy-five thousand people in two years! Two years! How many more people have to die before his bosses finally say, "Dennis, you were right all along."

Instead, they said Dennis had turned the case into a personal vendetta and he was taken off the trial. Now he worked in Medical Device compliance, making sure the newest tongue depressors and cotton balls put in their paperwork properly.

With his morning completely ruined by Galloway, whom he refused to call Tripp, he turned off the TV and went to feed his precious Snowflake. What did Tripp stand for anyways? It sounded ridiculous. Snowflake hopped onto the counter and started purring. She knew it was breakfast time. Dennis stroked his cat for a minute and said to no one in particular, "He better not try any other trials because it won't fly with me one bit." Snowflake meowed loudly in agreement or maybe because Dennis stopped petting her. Looking at the clock, Dennis quickened his pace, so he would not be late. He grabbed the keys to his Mini Cooper, kissed his cat on the head, and rushed to the door.

WEST ORANGE, NEW JERSEY

"Can we go the easy way?" Cassie Elm asked her husband, Terry, as they ran their normal route through the neighborhood. Cassie and

Terry were both avid runners, but Cassie had decided that taking the hard way was not in the works for her this Friday morning. She thought she was coming down with a cold and the hills of West Orange were unforgiving.

Terry, hyper-competitive, yelled, "Race you!" With a curse under her breath, she took off after him. She hated when he did this, but if she didn't compete he would hog the shower and she'll be late to work.

As Terry chugged up the hill, Cassie veered off and ran through her neighbors' yards, cutting the route diagonally. Two sprinklers and a fence later, she ended up at her front door with Terry nowhere in sight. She opened the door and was in the shower before Terry reached the driveway.

Terry, panting and very confused as to how Cassie beat him, flopped on the couch and flipped on the TV. Munching on the power bar he grabbed from the kitchen, he flipped through the channels. He landed on Lee Goldberg talking to some guy. *How does Lee Goldberg have more hair than me?* Terry thought in passing. Terry's bald spot has grown so much that he started shaving his head.

Still munching on the bar, Terry continued to watch while waiting for Cassie to get out of the shower. *Maybe I should join her in the shower? Wait, the last time I did that we were both late to work ... still worth it.*

As Terry swung himself forward, he took off his drenched t-shirt and started to walk upstairs when he stopped. *Did the guy just say what I think he said?* Going back to the TV, he rewound the feed and played it again. Lee Goldberg asked the question, "Do you think you'll be able to cure other diseases like sickle cell?"

The guy, who Terry assumed is a doctor, answered with an affirmative and mentioned cystic fibrosis (CF) as a good candidate. That is what Terry heard. This guy could maybe cure CF. Terry and Cassie decided not to have children because they were both carriers of the CF gene. CF is a disease that causes you to build up mucus in your lungs and makes breathing very difficult. The lives of people with CF is hard and the life expectancy is much shorter than the average human. Since they are both carriers, their potential children would have a 25 percent chance of being born with CF. A one in four shot of having a child die before age forty wasn't good odds for them. Terry and Cassie didn't think they were strong enough to potentially watch their children actually drown to death. There were certainly ways to have children but the couple had decided a long time ago that they would simply have each other.

They had grappled with the idea for a long time. All of the alternative options were either risky, painful or expensive. Adoption was expensive. Fertility treatments were expensive and could be painful for Cassie. Trying to have a baby naturally was too risky.

Could this doctor give them the chance to have children? Terry took down the name of the doctor, Allen Galloway, and raced upstairs to catch the end of that shower. He'd have to look up Dr. Galloway at work.

LUDLOW, MISSISSIPPI

Jodi-Ann Kapp almost burned the bacon. "Oh shit, oh shit, oh shit," she muttered under her breath. She saved half of it with a sigh. She was going to have to make more grits to compensate. Jodi-Ann was flabbergasted, hence, the burnt bacon. Lee Goldberg, who Jodi-Ann thought was quite handsome for a news anchor, had just asked the doctor if he would change babies before they were born.

The doctor said yes!

She could not believe that on God's green Earth, they let a doctor edit a person's DNA. It sounded sacrilegious. Mrs. Kapp firmly believed that God created every person, no matter what, in his likeness. It wasn't our job to change that.

While Jodi dealt with those thoughts and the grits, Calvin Kapp sauntered down the stairs. He worked for the Park Service and was never in a hurry. Thank God his wife helped get him ready every day. What would he do without her?

"Mornin' baby, how are ya?" Calvin said with an easy southern accent.

"I do not know Cal, I do not know. I was watching *The Today Show* and you know what they said? A doctor changed people's DNA LEGALLY and took away their blood disease. Can you imagine that? It's just not right."

Cal could tell that his wife was getting worked up again. Ever since Jimmy was born, she was always worried about health things. Trying to be helpful, Tony goes, "Ain't that a good thing Jo? They are all better. Could he do it for Jimmy?"

"Do not say those types of things in front of him! Jimmy is fine just how God created him. It isn't his fault anyways. It was the MMR and you know it," Jodi proclaimed.

Jodi-Ann allowed the doctor to give Jimmy the MMR vaccine and then, Jimmy couldn't speak. She refused to give Leila any vaccines, and she was normal.

The doctors tried their best to tell Jodi-Ann that he wasn't speaking before the vaccines, that it was in his genes and he was born that way. She knew it was a bold faced lie. The pharmaceutical companies had poisoned her son with Mercury and Cyanide. She was sure of it.

She had read on the Internet that the heavy metals given to the children through the vaccines changes their brains and that is what causes the autism. It made too much sense to not be true.

Cal had struck a nerve again. Finishing his grits, he got up from the table and walked over to his wife. She was looking at the kids. Jodi-Ann would not have that talk in her house and Cal knew it. He just desperately wanted a normal son. Jimmy was born with a non-verbal form of Autism. The boy was six years old and barely said anything. They got excited when he said "dog" last Spring. Jimmy was currently playing on the living room floor with some blocks with his sister. Leila was four years old and wouldn't stop talking. Cal wrapped his arms around Jodi and put his lips on her head.

"Baby, you know I didn't mean anything by it. I'm sorry and you're right, Jimmy is fine the way he is."

With that, he kissed her one more time, grabbed his turkey sandwich and sweet tea, and hopped in his truck.

Jodi continued to look at her children. Why would people want to change their DNA? It sounded dangerous. It's unholy. As she thought about it more, the anger kept brewing. If everyone was perfect, what would happen to kids like Jimmy? They'd be cast aside and never get the chance to live a normal life. So what if he couldn't talk? He could be really good at other things.

Jodi couldn't let that happen. She would need to do something for Jimmy's sake. Jodi went to do the dishes and made herself a promise. Jimmy would not be cast aside by that so-called Dr. Perfect.

III.

13 DECEMBER 2025

NEW YORK, NEW YORK

MORTI ACTUALLY ENJOYED CHRISTMAS. Standing amongst friends, clad in various shades of red and green, he sipped his drink casually. He was on call for today, meaning his drink was of the non-alcoholic variety. He couldn't be dropping babies due to partying.

Caught up in conversation, a colleague turned and looked at Morti. "So, how does it feel being one of the two hottest doctors in New York City right now?"

"Oh, can it. You know very well that I will never be on TV. They don't let cranky doctors like me on the morning shows. That's Tripp's job."

"Cut the shit Morti, I know you're loving this."

"Honestly, it's been okay. I could get way more work done without all of the attention. We're getting a lot of good and bad press. Pretty contentious."

Another doctor chimed in, "I get that, you all are swimming in pretty ethically murky waters."

Morti knew where this was going, "I know. A lot of people don't like the idea but honestly if we can help people have more meaningful lives, then I don't see the harm. I'm not making people have three eyes or something."

"You could though," the doctor chimed in, wagging his finger at Morti. "That's the scary part."

"When I discover the gene for large appendages, I'll be sure to call you last," Morti said with a wry smile.

Morti's wife sauntered over to the group. "What are you three laughing about? Causing trouble in the corner, being anti-social."

Morti kissed his wife on the head, bringing her into the group. "We were actually just talking about the clinical trial and how Tim here thinks we should move into the penis enlargement business."

"I imagine there is probably a large market for that. Could you imagine, you all take out the plastic surgery market by just changing the genes! All of those Los Angeles doctors would be out of a job!"

The group laughed at that one.

"Next, you'll be changing eye and hair colors. Everyone will be tall, dark and handsome," one person commented.

"Well, not you Morti. You'll always be short and ugly," Tim, the other doctor jabbed.

"Shut up Tim, like you should talk." Morti and Tim were the same height.

"Aw, babe, it's okay, I still love you," Morti's wife said playfully.

As the conversation continued with light-hearted ribbing and jokes, Morti thought to himself about those plastic surgeons. *It would be hilarious to watch them all lose their business.*

He could imagine the slogan now, "Perfect People, Born that Way."

IV.

SLAVOMIR WAS DRIPPING WITH SWEAT. THAT last hook hurt like a bitch. He was starting to wonder if he was getting old.

Training with Alex, a full ten years his junior, was getting to be more trouble than it was worth. Twice a week for the last five years, Alex and Arkady took turns stepping into the ring with Slavomir. He refused to be considered old and needed to keep in shape for his sparring matches with Putin.

Slavomir and Alex circled each other like dogs in a ring. Alex and Arkady were also former Spetsnaz, making them as lethal as Slavomir. He also demanded that they both keep their instincts sharp. This job was not some cushy gig, like babysitting diplomat's children. If they wanted something like that, they would have to look for employment elsewhere.

Alex, sensing Slavomir was rattled by his last attempt, stepped forward and grabbed for Slavomir's shirt. Slavomir stepped in at the same time as Alex and threw a wicked elbow, landing it squarely below

Alex's left eye socket. With his grip firmly clasped on Slavomir, Alex stumbled back.

A right leg sweep landed both of them on the ground in a cluster-fuck of legs and arms. Scrambling for dominance, Slavomir slammed his head into the chest of Alex while splaying his legs out to avoid the Russian's arms. Alex, clearly angered by the turn of events, mercilessly pounded on Slavomir's head as if banging on a table.

Slavomir quickly tucked his legs underneath him while keeping his arms wrapped around the burly Russian. Bleeding from a cut on his face, Slavomir threw his legs up in the air and behind him. Using the momentum, he drove his knee into Alex's ribcage, cracking a rib.

"You piece of shit!" screamed Alex as he struggled to breath.

At this point, Arkady entered the room.

Slavomir, seeing Arkady, placed a hand on Alex's face and pushed himself up.

"Good match," Slavomir said with a smile.

"Go fuck yourself," replied Alex. Both Alex and Arkady were never professional with their boss. They had earned that right through their similar military backgrounds and loyalty. Otherwise, that type of disrespect would never fly.

Arkady had to admit, his boss was a tough bastard. He took one look at Alex, insulted his manhood and passed a manila folder to Slavomir. Both fighters were bleeding and drenched in sweat. It apparently was a good match.

Slavomir, while wiping the blood off of his face, perused the file. Arkady had done a good job. The brief on this Dr. Galloway, or as the file said, Tripp, was quite thorough. Arkady had previously done intelligence work and it showed. It contained family history, finances, known associates, aliases, digital copies of his last interviews, known real-estate holdings and even school transcripts. It also showed the doctor loved coffee and was single. A man that was dedicated to his work.

"Can we trust the doctor?" asked Slavomir.

"The profile makes me think he will comply if we approach gently. No threats of violence. I would go with the change the world approach. Not money," offered Arkady.

Slavomir had taught his bodyguards to think in three ways. Money, power and violence. Every person will eventually cave due to those three things. Arkady was suggesting they go with the power approach. Slavomir kept looking at the file and nodded. He would have to make up his mind later. First, he had lunch with the Minister of Commerce in an hour.

"Find out when a vacation to New York would suit Anna. I want to meet with this doctor," ordered Slavomir. With that, he walked off the mats to shower and eat.

V.

AIDEN HAD GOTTEN TO THE RESTAURANT AT 8:45 a.m. in the morning. He wanted to make sure they got the table in the back section against the wall, so they wouldn't be disturbed. As the trial manager and a slew of other titles, meeting coordination fell under his responsibilities. Standing at about five feet six inches and one hundred thirty pounds with spiky blonde hair and chiseled cheekbones, Aiden looked like what every basic college girl that moved to New York wanted to look like. He had the smarts of a Goldman banker and the looks of a Williamsburg bartender. And sure enough he combined those skills to become the right hand man of the most famous doctors currently living in fucking Manhattan. As soon as Teresa came to the hostess stand, he instantly turned on the charm.

They traded Manhattan gossip for a few minutes before she led them to their normal spot. Aiden felt bad for the girl. She flirted with him so badly and she still couldn't figure it out. She wasn't the smartest girl in New York.

32

Slapping his leather bomber onto a chair, he sent out the agenda for today's meeting and ordered the requisite drinks. Six coffees, two orange juices and one chocolate milk. Tony came from the gym and said, "He needed the protein."

Aiden thought that Tony was a child.

Tony showed up first, Tripp and Morti third and the girls trailing behind. Tony smelled like shit while the girls were in their weekend wear: sweatpants and messy buns. They both smelled of Tequila. Aiden had to admit, Tripp and Morti always looked good. Morti was draped in Ralph Lauren corduroys and a pink dress shirt while Tripp was in dark jeans and a Patagonia fleece. When everyone was settled, Aiden began the meeting.

"So, mornin' everyone, you have the agendas in your emails; let's get through this so we can enjoy our weekends. Dr. Stein, you have two interviews and a lecture at Princeton this week; I put them in our calendar. Dr. Galloway, you are at an Infertility symposium Thursday through Saturday but we will still have our meeting next week. Michelle, don't roll your eyes. Tony, we have to on-board the new techs and have another thirty cell lines due between Monday and Wednesday. Girls, I need the inventories by Tuesday, if we want the stuff to get here by Friday. Any questions?"

Tara, feeling nauseous from the night before just moaned but Michelle spoke up.

"I received an email from a ... Terry Elm. He or she, I don't really know. They mentioned their wife, but I don't think that tells us anything anymore, want to have a kid but they are both carriers of the ... CF gene. He mentions something ... uhh ... exon 4? Does that mean anything to you guys? Anyways, they wanted to know if you two could help."

Aiden hadn't expected queries so quickly. In the executive meeting, Tripp and Morti had mentioned looking for viable diseases to expand to, but they were not supposed to start for another year at least. They had over sixty-five thousand lines to still convert for sickle cell and needed to expand their facilities substantially before even thinking about diversifying.

Morti spoke first, "We've talked about this before but are we ready to start another trial? I don't think we could."

Aiden agreed with Morti but held his tongue before speaking. Tony unfortunately did not.

"I think we should say fuck it and go for it. We've got some serious momentum right now Doc."

Aiden didn't disagree but it was not in his nature to agree with Tony. He would rather eat a dick than agree with Tony. Overall, Aiden found Tony competent but annoying. Very annoying.

Morti and Tony went back and forth for a minute or two as everyone placed their food orders. Tripp was very excited about his co-op platter with sausage gravy. It came with thick cut bacon, biscuits, eggs, hash browns and that beloved gravy. While ordering his second cup of coffee (third of the day), Tripp chimed in.

"Could we use them for a proof of concept for the next trial?"

Technically, the platform they were using had already been approved for a utility process patent. They would just need to show that it would work in cystic fibrosis as well for the FDA to give the go ahead. That would mean some sort of proof of concept test, which is generally done in a Phase II or IIa study.

The trials that Dr. Stein and Galloway were conducting fell into a hazy regulatory area to say the least. Being on the cutting edge of science can be difficult to navigate from a regulatory perspective. They had their process patent, so they were the only people that could do the technique, but the FDA regulated the products. The diseases they were tackling were also considered orphan diseases, meaning that the population sizes were very small. Orphan disease could get quicker reviewing periods by the FDA, if they qualified. Aiden, being the clinical trial manager, was considered the river guide and the clinical trial process was a river filled with waterfalls and rapids.

"I don't think a traditional proof of concept is the way to go. I think the FDA will shut that one down. Maybe if we take an Orphan Disease approach, we could make it work," Aiden suggested.

Michelle, Tony and Tara all looked confused.

Aiden explained. "We all know that we work in Orphan Diseases, meaning there are less than two hundred thousand people in the United States with the disease. Both sickle cell and CF fall into that category. So by filling out the paperwork that goes along with Orphan Diseases, we may be able to get everything approved."

"Why do they separate Orphan Diseases from other diseases?" asked Michelle.

"Good Question. By separating them out, it allows the really sick people or people with no other alternatives to try drugs that aren't quite approved yet. It could also be used when a normal trial might not be the best option, like if the population size was very small," Aiden responded.

"We should be able to copy and paste from some of our previously approved applications," Tripp stated for the crowd.

"Yes, exactly. That should speed things up for us," Aiden added.

"This is why we let Aiden take off on Fridays," Dr. Stein said, grinning from ear to ear. The Friday Fiasco, as it had been dubbed by Dr. Galloway, happened every Friday. Michelle and Tara would come in hungover, Tony would cover for them and Aiden would disappear, with permission of course.

Tripp really liked the idea. It could work. Getting it past Myers, the FDA reviewer from their last trial would be a real pain in the ass. If he found out that we were submitting another trial so soon, he would definitely want to be a reviewer. Maybe a call to the head of the Center for Biologics Evaluation and Research, the department that would handle their case, would be in order. That guy was so sensitive for absolutely no reason.

"After this Morti and I will stay and talk. Michelle, don't answer that email yet, but don't fucking delete it either. If we can come to a decision, Morti will brief you next Saturday and we will move from there."

With that, the meeting was over. Everyone topped off their coffees and finished their meals. Tripp ordered another side of biscuits and gravy for later, along with another coffee. Morti sipped his orange juice and stared at Tripp.

"What?" asked Tripp. He hated when Morti did the staring thing.

"I can see you thinking; you don't do it very often. It looks painful."

"Are you even supposed to be here? It is Saturday you know," Tripp quipped.

The bantering continued until Morti decided enough was enough. Describing what he would do to Tripp's sister was getting a little vulgar.

"So, about the CF thing, what do you think? I think it could work. I just think we are spread a little too thin right now. We have five new techs coming on Monday and are upping our production quotas a lot. Also, we have to move the labs by April," Morti said.

Morti was right. They probably wouldn't start the process until April anyways and the paperwork alone would take three months initially. "How about this? We hire a Regulatory person to help Aiden and lighten his load a little. We could begin the process in April, if we like the patients and see how it plays out. I imagine you and I wouldn't be doing anything except signing forms and having meetings until 2028 at the earliest," Tripp said.

"Is this about Hal?" Morti asked gingerly. He knew that Tripp's brother was sensitive but didn't want business and family life to get mixed up.

"You know it is," Tripp said. "If we could get this done, that would be another foundation out of business!" Putting disease foundations out of business was a by-product of their work, much to the dismay of the foundation executives.

Morti, the skeptical one of the two, thought for a moment while staring into his orange juice. He wasn't going to laugh at Tripp's blunt attempt at covering up his family history. He just swirled his orange juice and sighed. Tripp gave him some time and sipped his coffee.

After a few moments, Morti looked up and said, "I'm not doing anything until 2028."

Tripp, knowing they had come to conclusion, tilted his cup to the ceiling and let out a breath. The next stop was CF.

15 JANUARY 2026

WEST ORANGE, NEW JERSEY

It was Chinese food night. General Tso's, pork fried rice, dumplings and lo mein lined the kitchen island as Terry and Cassie chowed down. Although Cassie is a health fanatic about what she eats, her one weakness is Thursday Chinese food. Classic Pop fills the air while they talk about their days. Terry works in masonry while Cassie works as a consultant.

As they were talking, the musician, Mr. James Bay, or as Cassie calls him, Mr. Mysterious, is interrupted by a ding from Gmail. Terry gets up from the table to close out his account. They have a rule that there can be no electronics at the dinner table because Terry would never put down his phone if the rule wasn't in place. As he went to log out, he stopped.

"Honey, come over here. I got an email from Dr. Galloway's office."

Cassie leaves her stool and wraps her arms around his shoulders to read.

Re: Inquiry
Galloway and Stein Reproductive Associates
to Terry Elm

Dear Mr. Elm,

We are writing in response to your inquiry of Dr. Galloway and Steins' services. At this time, the techniques utilized by Dr. Galloway and Dr. Stein are only permitted for the treatment and curing of sickle cell anemia, otherwise known as sickle cell disease or SCD.

Both Dr. Galloway and Dr. Stein would like to inform you that they cannot help immediately. They do wish that you would schedule an appointment with the office in order to discuss a potential opportunity that they believe would be beneficial. Please call us during business hours to set up your appointment at our Lower West Side office in New York, New York.

Thank you and we look forward to meeting with you.

Sincerely,
Aiden McDonald
Office Manager, Galloway and Stein Reproductive Associates
New York, New York

"Holy shit are we going to get a baby?" Terry asked. His heart was racing.

"I don't know but I don't want to get my hopes up," Cassie said.

"I know but if we can make this happen, it could be awesome," Terry said.

"I know but let's play it cool for now. It still may be financially out of reach." Cassie was always the cautious one.

With a nod, Terry hugged Cassie. He was determined to make this happen for her. He had reignited the idea of children and now he had to make it happen.

VI.

CASSIE WAS NERVOUS. BUNDLED IN HER olive parka, gloves and Bean boots, she could still feel the cold digging into her soul. Terry stood beside her, looking up at the nondescript brick building that potentially held their future. She reached out and intertwined her fingers with his. His hands, enveloping hers in a warm cocoon, made her feel a bit more comfortable with what is to come.

Terry turned to his wife, who looked like a Yeti at this point, and asked, "You ready?"

She nodded, almost hesitantly, as if saying yes was a bad thing. Seeing the nervousness radiate through her, he tugged her in close, kissed her on the head and led her to the front door. Walking through the glass, they were immediately hit with the artificial heat. It was almost too hot. Cassie and Terry immediately started peeling off layers as they looked around. Seeing a sign, Cassie perused the names while removing her scarf and gloves until she landed on what she was looking for.

Galloway and Stein Reproductive Associates Suite 501

Cassie, pressing the elevator button, turned back to Terry, who was still struggling with his layers. "Top floor it is."

Finally done adjusting his sweater, he gave her a wink and stepped up to await the ride.

Moving quickly, the elevator came to a stop on the fifth floor. Opening up into a small entryway, they stepped out of the elevator and immediately moved through a pair of glass doors. Inside the doors, they were greeted with the smell of lavender. Looking around the waiting room, Cassie's thoughts were running rampant. *I think this is the nicest waiting room I've ever been in. Those chairs are nicer than the ones in our living room.*

Cassie wasn't wrong. The walls, the color of a gentle sea, were offset by mahogany wainscoting. The chairs, brown leather, sat upon a plush navy carpet, giving off the vibe of a private dining club instead of a doctor's office. Hanging on the walls were degrees from Harvard, Boston University, Rutgers University and Columbia. Magazine and news articles were also framed, the photos showing a pair of men, beaming with pride that Cassie could only assume were Dr. Stein and Galloway.

Giving them a second to adjust, Tara greeted them warmly. "Good Morning, did you guys find the office okay?"

"Yes it wasn't too bad, pretty easy actually," Terry said as Tara started putting a clipboard together.

"Great, what's the last name?" Tara asked with warm professionalism. She hated how fake she had to be at work. It was painful. Michelle and her oftentimes tried to get each other to break character by saying ridiculous things. Michelle was on break. The guy was a cutie too, so that helped make it easier. He reminded her of her college boyfriend. Maybe she would reach out to that guy.

"The last name is Elm. Cassie and Terry Elm," Cassie said quickly.

Clicking the name into the computer, Tara quickly realized this couple was a big deal. Tara snapped back to reality. No flirting with the clinical trial couple. "Okay great, Cassie and Terry. Dr. Galloway and Stein are excited to meet with you. Here is a clipboard that we ask all of our patients to fill out. It's a confidentiality waiver, health forms for both of you, insurance information and family history forms. You will be meeting with the whole team today, so don't be shocked when you see the conference room. You guys are going to be great."

Cassie gave a smile and wondered what she meant by the whole team. Terry and Cassie sunk into a pair of seats and began to fill out the paperwork. Cassie always thought it was funny when fancy places used cheap pens. She thought the juxtaposition between ornate and common place was funny.

About halfway through the small stack of paperwork, a stocky Asian guy with an octopus tattoo on his forearm came out from the hallway laughing. He was yelling something over his shoulder when he turned the corner and saw the couple. The nurse gave him a dirty look, which he quickly returned. He quickly grabbed a butterscotch dum-dum from the front desk and asked the couple, "Hey do you guys want a lollipop? We have every flavor under the sun!"

Cassie quickly said no. She was too nervous. Terry got up with his finished paperwork and looked at the dum-dums. The Asian guy whispered something to the nurse. Her response, which Terry overheard, was, "Tell 'em yourself, big boy."

Tony, never shy with patients, said a little too loudly, "No problem. Good Morning, I'm Tony, head cell culture supervisor. I'm one of the people you'll be meeting with today. The docs are getting set up in the conference room and said to let you know that they're ready when you're all set with the paperwork."

Terry and Tony shook hands and Tony gave Cassie a small wave. The poor girl was shaking in her boots. Swiping another butterscotch, Tony turned to the back and jogged down the hallway.

After another minute of paperwork, Cassie stood up and placed her information on the front desk. The nurse gave everything the once-over and asked if the couple was ready to go. Terry placed his hand on Cassie's shoulder and gave it a gentle squeeze. They followed the nurse down a hallway past what looked like examination rooms and a lab with a couple of people working. One person, seeing the couple, gave a pleasant smile as she was holding a couple of blood tubes.

The nurse opened a door and let the couple pass. Inside the room was a large wooden table and more comfortable leather chairs. Surrounding the table was a small group. A woman who looked like the first nurse's twin, the Asian guy named Tony, a very blonde New York man, and the two doctors. Everyone stood up practically at the same time.

The shorter doctor, wearing a peach button down and navy slacks, walked over to the couple and shook both their hands. "Good Morning, my name is Dr. Stein, welcome, please take a seat. Do you want anything to drink? Coffee, soda, water? Something stronger?"

"I would take a water, if you have it," Cassie said sheepishly.

"Sparkling or Flat?" the first nurse asked.

"Flat is fine thanks."

The nurse left the conference room and came back with a glass and a bottle of water. Cassie thanked the nurse while she sat down next to her look-alike. The taller doctor, with a green button down shirt, brown corduroys and a grey V-neck sweater began the meeting.

"Good Morning, thanks for taking the time today to come in and talk with us. Let me start with introductions. My name is Allen Galloway and I'm an infertility specialist. My colleague, Dr. Stein, is a geneticist by trade but also an OB-GYN. You've already met Tara; she will be the point of contact through our time together. I believe you already met Tony. Finally, we have Michelle, who is one of our clinical trial nurses and Aiden, who is our clinical trial manager. We are all super excited that you reached out to us. So, I know Aiden sent you all an email but how about you tell us how you heard about us and what brought you to reach out."

Cassie looked at Terry, signaling that he should do the talking. Terry, taking the cue, sat up a little bit straighter and began.

"Well Cassie and I had just got back from a run and she kicked my ass. So, I was waiting for the shower when I saw your interview on *The Today Show*. You had mentioned that you may be able to cure other diseases, and you mentioned cystic fibrosis. Cassie and I are both carriers for CF and we didn't want to take the chances of one of our kids having CF and we couldn't really afford a fertility specialist. We wanted kids but the risks were too great for us. So, when I saw your interview, I did some research and said, 'What the fuck could I lose?' Ya know?"

Cassie smacked him in the arm for the language. Clearly, she wanted him on his best behavior.

Tony and Michelle laughed while Dr. Galloway smirked. Dr. Stein, sensing Cassie's embarrassment, only said one more thing the whole meeting, "That's a fucking good story."

Terry chuckled while Cassie let out a little laugh. Aiden, who at this point hadn't said a word, chimed in.

"We have an offer we'd like to lay out for you. First off, I just want to confirm, Cassie you are twenty-five years old and Terry you are twenty-seven years old?"

Cassie, finding her voice, said, "That's correct."

Aiden, seemingly happy with the response, continued, "That's great. Our timeline is a little extended, so we wanted to make sure we had some running room. So, do you know how clinical trials work?"

Cassie and Terry both shook their heads.

"Okay that's fine. So, when you go to get a drug approved, you have to submit a bunch of paperwork that shows that the drug is safe, more effective than what is out there and novel. You also need to show the drug is not toxic and conduct animal studies, in addition to testing on humans. Those parts of a clinical trial are broken out into phases called Phase I, II and III. We need to submit all of this paperwork, specifically something called a Biologics License Application, because we would be using your altered blood as a drug. Testing your altered blood on you would be classified as a phase III event. Now normally, this process would take eight years in a phase III study, but we are looking to cut it down significantly through some, uh, sneaky but legal loopholes."

Terry, suddenly suspicious, jumped at that pause, "What sneaky loopholes are we talking about here? I don't need the government on my ass."

Aiden raised his hands in a 'don't shoot' fashion, feigning surrender. "I promise you it is all legal. We plan on working with the FDA to use our sickle cell data for phase I and II. We would have to prove we could edit your blood, but that shouldn't be a problem. Tony is a magician when it comes to DNA editing. The sneaky part is where we actually remove the CF gene from your blood. We are going to do a phase IIa study at the same time as the phase II, so we should be able to treat you in three years."

"How is that possible? You just said humans get tested in phase III," Cassie asked.

Dr. Galloway stepped in to field the question, "We would be submitting a BLA like Aiden said, but it would be a special BLA due to the fact that cystic fibrosis is an Orphan Disease, meaning that not many people in the United States have the gene. If we get the orphan disease rating, the clinical trials will get more attention and move quicker, in hope to save lives more quickly, or in your case, get you a baby."

Terry and Cassie looked at each other. They were talking in years now instead of weeks. Although they weren't sure what to expect, it still hurt to think they could not have a baby until Terry was passed thirty years old. That wasn't old, but three years seemed like a lifetime. It was tough on them mentally, switching from a "never baby" mindset to a "maybe baby" mindset.

Cassie turned to Tony and asked, "How would you cure us? You are the DNA magician right?"

Tony, still sucking on the butterscotch dum-dum, popped the lollipop out of his mouth and in one breath said, "Yes ma'am, that's correct. What we would do is take a bone marrow sample, and I'm not going to lie, that hurts a little, create your own stem cells and edit the DNA using a platform called CRISPR/Cas9. From there, we create more of the new DNA and through a full bone marrow transfusion, replace your old DNA with the new DNA. Your bone marrow differentiates into the rest of your body cells and you eventually lose all of your old DNA through the natural turnover process. So, I will personally do the stem cell propagation and editing. From there, a transplant surgeon, who you would meet eventually, would take my handy work and replace the old with the new. Boom-shaka-laka, no more CF."

At that point, Tony took another breath and put the dum-dum back in his mouth.

"That easy huh? And why couldn't we edit our baby instead?" Terry said, still suspicious.

"For me it is sir, I have two Master's degrees in cell biology and helped Dr. Tripp and Morti with the whole process from start to finish. This is my baby. To answer your second question, we aren't approved to use the technique in children or embryos at this time," Tony said proudly. This time he did not remove the lollipop.

There it was again, Tripp thought. *How come everyone keeps asking about the embryos? Is there a market there that we are missing? It would be way too expensive and risky. Imagine the fallout if something, an editing mistake, happened in a fetus. Spontaneous abortions do not look good. But maybe, just maybe, I should do some more research.*

Tripp, done with his thoughts, chimed back in, "This process is going to be long, difficult and there are going to be a lot of people trying to stop this process. In our sickle cell trial, we had a lot of opposition within the FDA. Now, because we have gotten a lot of external attention, we will see what type of heat we get. We riled up some conservative circles with our last announcement. Now, we don't want to discourage you, in fact, quite the opposite. We are prepared to go to war for you. We just want to make sure that you, A, understand everything that is going on and, B, what it all entails."

Cassie and Terry once again looked at each other. Cassie asked, "Can we have a minute?"

Tripp said, "Of course," and everyone stood and left the room. Once everyone was gone, Cassie grabbed Terry's hand and started.

"What do you think? It seems risky, and they said the FDA might deny this whole thing. Also, how do we ensure the baby doesn't get CF? I still don't get it," Cassie said.

Terry took a moment to think. Making a decision now seemed a little hasty. He didn't like to rush into these types of things.

"Well they seemed pretty upfront about everything. If the FDA denies us, we're back right where we started. If it passes, we get to have a baby. I'm thinking that they are going to pay for it too, but we should double check that. Also, yea, that's a good question," Terry said.

"So, if they are going to pay for it, and we double check everything, go for the ride?" Cassie asked, hopeful.

Terry kissed her long and hard. It was one of those kisses that tries to convey complex emotions through one gesture. He wanted her to know how he felt but just didn't have the words to express himself. They broke apart and looked at each other for a minute.

"I love you," he said, and then went to the door. "We're ready for you guys."

The team came back into the room and looked at the couple.

Terry cut the tension quickly. "How do we make sure our baby doesn't have CF?"

Tripp chimed in, "Great question! We should have answered that first. Through editing your DNA Terry, the baby won't be able to actually get the CF disease. The baby may inherit the gene from Cassie, but that won't matter."

"So, in reality, only Terry needs to have the procedure?" Cassie asked.

"Correct, but potentially we would also like to edit yours as well. We will have to discuss. We want Cassie enrolled in the trial just in case, even if she ends up being a negative control," Morti said.

Terry thought that was sufficient. "We're in, if you're paying. I would personally like to keep our names out of the paper as long as we can. We just want a fuckin' baby. Babe, you want to say anything?"

Cassie quoted her husband by saying, "I guess we are going balls to the wall. So what's next?"

The group laughed. Even Aiden, who had been stoic throughout the meeting, let out a chuckle.

"So we start with a ton of blood work and DNA sequencing to confirm your genetic diagnosis. We will start the IND process on our end. Finally, we will meet quarterly until we begin the treatment process, and at that point we will meet much more frequently," Aiden said.

He was anxious to get everything started. It was a large ordeal.

Michelle stepped out and brought back a bottle of champagne and a bottle of Iced Tea with neon notes attached.

Michelle explained, "So we have a tradition here at the office, that whenever we take on a new project, we write a note to the disease on a bottle of champagne. If we achieve the goal, we get to drink the bottle. In your case, achieving the goal might mean that Cassie is pregnant, so we decided that a bottle of Iced Tea might be a good idea too. Just to let you know, the last message to sickle cell was, and I quote, 'Fuck you sickle cell. Love, The Team.'"

Michelle then handed over two felt-tip markers to Terry and Cassie and said, "We want you to write the message."

Terry took the champagne and passed the Iced Tea to Cassie as if the bottles themselves were infants. After a minute of intense thought, Terry started scribbling. His face scrunched at the brow as he wrote every word with care. After watching him for a second, Cassie followed suit. What we had left was the beginning of a huge undertaking:

On the Champagne bottle:

"Dear Cystic Fibrodick,
You weren't strong enough to get us and you sure as fuck are not getting our kid. Blow us.
Love,
The Team"

On the Tea:

"Dear Cystic Fibrosis,
You tried to take away my child's future. Now I'm going to take yours. May you burn in Hell.
Warm Regards,
The Team."

VII.

AIDEN WAS IN ABSOLUTELY NO MOOD TO flirt with Teresa today. In fact, he was in no mood to be at this meeting. There were much bigger things he should be doing, like figuring out how Tripp and Morti were going to pay for their salaries, a brand new clinical trial, a lab expansion and the salaries of all the other schmucks they kept hiring. His last priority was ordering coffee and orange juices before the team showed up.

Sensing something was amiss, Teresa, trying to be sweet, asked, "You okay Aiden? You seem off today. Can I get you something?"

"Yea actually, can you tell our waiter I think he's got a great ass and get me a screwdriver? Actually make it a double. Thanks."

Aiden had decided that there would be no more flirting with the hot-air balloon that was this girl.

Teresa, shocked, fumbled on what Aiden thought was the word 'sure' and disappeared as the team rolled in. Tony, Michelle and Tara had gone out the night before and it showed. Michelle was as pale as Aiden was.

Tara spoke first while flopping into her chair, "Can we order drinks, I need this headache to go away."

"Sure, what the fuck, I already ordered one," Aiden said with a sass that was generally only used with annoying sales reps.

Morti came in shortly after, holding a glass of orange juice.

"Teresa said this was for you but she looked a little upset," Morti said with questioning eyes.

Aiden, ignored the unspoken question and took a large gulp of his double screwdriver.

Lastly, Tripp sauntered to the back of the restaurant. He sat next to Aiden while simultaneously smelling the vodka that Tony was sweating. Apparently, it had been a good night.

"Don't you all look wide-eyed and bushy-tailed," quipped Tripp. He loved mocking them when they were too incapacitated to function.

Aiden, wanting desperately to get back to the office, started immediately. "Okay listen up, I don't have much time. We make the move into the new lab space Monday. Tony, you coordinate that. The following Monday I am supposed to have the pre-IND paperwork in and set up a meeting down in Silver Spring. I expect you Tony, and Tripp and Morti to be at that meeting. I will forward you the date when I have it."

"How is the paperwork going?" asked Morti.

"Not well, I basically have to redo a lot of the preliminary analysis work because the mutations are obviously different in CF than in sickle cell," Aiden said. "Having to explain the necessity of the treatments based on previous research appears to be a challenge."

Aiden had mentioned this before, but it was ignored.

"Okay, I will help you with that this week," Tripp said. His schedule was lighter than Morti's this week anyways.

"Great, thanks, and we have to decide if Tara or Michelle is moving to the new lab. This is the last major point," Aiden said. He was trying to end this meeting now.

Tony chimed in, "Michelle comes with me to the lab; she knows the shipping processes like the back of her hand."

Michelle, barely awake, said, "If that's okay with *mi amor*, and she can *viva sin mio*. It's okay with me. Adios lover."

Tara began to fake cry as Tony fake rubbed her back. Aiden was over it and began to pack up.

Tripp spoke up, "Hey where are you going? We haven't even ordered breakfast yet?"

"I've got to find some more funding for everything. We're going to be tight."

"How tight?" Morti asked.

"Tighter than Tony's gym spandex. I don't know how we are going to fund the trial with the expansion and the new people coming on," Aiden confessed. He was going to tell the doc in private, but they had asked. *C'est la vie.*

"Should I get on the phone with some VCs?" Tripp asked.

Aiden sat back down but didn't take off his jacket. He still had a ton of work to do. "I would call everyone you know. In the next two years we are going to need another couple million or so. Maybe contact J&J again."

J&J or Johnson and Johnson was the pharmaceutical company that helped them fund the sickle cell clinical trial. Back in 2015 and 2016, J&J was going through a transitional phase and needed something in their pipeline desperately. It just so happened that Morti's uncle was VP of Development at J&J.

They began to chat on the first day of Chanukah and by the third, the deal was struck. J&J would receive a license on the editing platform, if the samples were run through Tripp and Morti's lab. That way they both won.

Morti stepped out with Aiden to make the call to his uncle. He needed to find out who the new VP of Development was. Hopefully, he wasn't an asshole.

1 APRIL 2026

NEW YORK, NEW YORK

Tripp, Morti and Aiden hopped off the conference call. As it turns out, SHE was an asshole. Krishna Patel, PhD and the current VP of Development at Johnson & Johnson, decided that cystic fibrosis was "not the target market that she saw the company going after" and that "the orphan drug market was pretty saturated." She also mentioned that she didn't particularly like Morti's uncle and that she would rather "drop dead then work with another Stein."

The mood within the conference room was morose. Tripp, seeing the metaphorical wall that he was hurtling toward get a lot closer, threw his legal pad across the room. The stress was getting to him. After Aiden had told them money was going to be tight, he took a look himself. Aiden was right; they are going to be short millions in the next couple of years. Their infertility clinic profits and the sickle cell cash flow wasn't enough to fund the new lab, a clinical trial and the office. Something had to give and apparently it wasn't going to be J and fucking J.

"What's our timeline?" Tripp asked Aiden. He needed to know how much wiggle room they had.

"I submit the pre-IND paperwork on the 6th and they have to put us on the calendar within ninety days. From there we have to have all of our paperwork in for them to review thirty days before the meeting. So, that puts us in the area of July," Aiden said.

"Okay, stick to the plan. I'll find the money. Even if we have to go public," Tripp assured his team.

Morti looked at him warily. He knew that was a bad idea but so did Tripp. Morti didn't need to give Tripp the warning glance. They had talked about it before the J&J deal for sickle cell but decided against it. *What choice do I have though?* thought Tripp. *If I can't get the money from private investors, I can get it from the people who think they have a shot at being cured. Pay and be saved! But we'll get railed by the FDA, if they find out we leaked it. You do not get your way by forcing the FDA's hand. Has crowdsourcing clinical trials ever happened before? I don't think so. Oh they are going to call me radical for sure. It's going to be tricky. I am in deep now. Real deep ...*

"Don't clue me in on that. if that's the path you take," Aiden said.

VIII.

JODI-ANN WAS CURLED UP ON THE LIVING room floor, hysterically crying. She had just gotten back from the grocery store. While trying to buy groceries, an old man came up to Jimmy and patted him on the head. The old man had commented that his grandson was never this good in the grocery store.

Jimmy, immediately after being touched, had a meltdown. He threw himself on the floor and wailed as if he was struck by the devil. It took Jodi a half hour to get him to the car and another twenty minutes to get him strapped into the car seat. A male manager had to carry Jimmy to the car because he wouldn't stop kicking and punching. That boy didn't stop wailing until they drove into the driveway. As soon as he was unleashed from the seat, he ran to his room and hid in the closet. He refused to come out.

Sitting on the floor, Jodi-Ann couldn't help but feel defeated. Jodi had tried everything to help her son. They enrolled him in special programs, constantly worked on his speech and went to meetings as far away as New Orleans. She had seen every doctor in the South. Everyone said the same thing: pray. To top it all off, that morning her girlfriend Patty had sent her an email talking about that Dr. Galloway again. Now, he was trying to cure cystic fibrosis.

Since Dr. Galloway's first trial was completed, conservatives and anti-vaccination advocates had rallied across the country for the work to stop. Several Congressman had stepped up to support the rallies, but no real change had come about. How could they stop the trials when people were being cured?

They couldn't and that was what scared Jodi. Her son couldn't get the help he needed now. She couldn't imagine how hard it would be, if everyone was healthy. Besides, changing your DNA was wrong. This doctor was doing the devil's bidding. How could the government not see that? The whole situation flabbergasted Jodi. She felt stuck between a rock and a hard place. She didn't have anywhere else to turn, so she turned to the Internet.

On every website she visited and every article she read, it said that vaccines were killing our children and that Dr. Galloway was going to do the same. Jodi was sure that he was putting heavy metals in people. He already killed one person in the trial! Dr. Galloway's representative said it was a labeling mistake but all of the websites said it wasn't. It was a practice run on inserting the heavy metals. The trial covered it up.

The tears rolling down Jodi's face slowed. She was having trouble breathing and couldn't cough and cry at the same time. Getting up from her floor, she reopened Patty's email and took another look.

Hi Jo,

Did you see that doctor who did the sickle cell trial is doing another one? This time he is doing cystic fibrosis. Dan Thomas from the County Republican Committee is holding a meeting to see who is interested in going to New York for a big rally. It's at 5:00 p.m. next Friday. I thought you would be interested since

we talked about him at Church a while ago. Let me know if you
go, so we can carpool!

TTYL,
Patty

1 JUNE 2026

SILVER SPRING, MARYLAND

No more cotton ball reviews for Dennis Myers. He had his feet up on his desk and was feeling himself today. Allen Galloway and Mortimer Stein had decided to be unconventional and that opened the door for Dennis to be back in the good graces of his superiors.

"The amount of gall those two have is really tremendous," Dennis said to himself while filing another excel sheet away. No one, no one ever, in the history of clinical trials, successfully raised enough money for a clinical trial online. Dennis would never admit to himself that it was actually impressive. He believed it was just another item to add to the list against Drs. Galloway and Stein.

His favorite mug, adorned with the Nan Porter quote, "If cats could talk, they wouldn't," was acting as a paper weight for his recently accessed filings from Galloway and Stein. Dennis had to prepare for their meeting and would not be caught off guard.

"I will not be caught off guard," Dennis mumbled to himself. He had already been yelled at today by his co-workers for talking to himself. It's the way he processes information, but his co-workers don't seem to understand.

6 JUNE 2026

NEW YORK, NEW YORK

Tripp was fucked. Really fucked. He sat on his couch, swirling his vodka and ginger ale. The golden, sparkling liquid didn't provide the comfort he needed, but it did numb him a little after the fourth. He knew that if this didn't work, he had a bottle of tequila in the freezer that would do the job.

He had eighteen days to come up with another one million five hundred thousand dollars. That would get them through the first couple of months of the trials. He thought for sure he would have until the end of June to find the money. For some fucked up reason, the FDA decided to schedule their meeting earlier than expected. It was a first in Tripp's book. The FDA rarely did anything early. They would need eight million dollars, give or take a million, to get through the end of phase IIa. That was to make sure Cassie and Terry could have their baby.

He hadn't told the couple that they might not have the funds. He couldn't bring himself, yet, to tell them. The last meeting they had, Cassie told them she bought baby clothes. Terry said he started thinking of names. It would kill them.

As Tripp continued to drown his brain cells in vodka, his doorbell rang.

Who the fuck is here so late? Tripp wondered. He really didn't want to be disturbed while getting painfully drunk.

Trudging to the door, he looked through the peephole to see three, very large men standing in front of his door. Tripp, being over six feet tall, never felt nervous around other tall people, but these guys seemed different.

"Can I help you?" asked Tripp through the door. He was not really sure what to do.

The man in the front of the group answered.

"Dr. Galloway, do you mind if I call you Tripp? My name is Slavomir Krukov and I'd like to talk to you about your practice."

How the fuck did this Russian guy know my name and where I live? What was his name again? This is like a fucking horror movie. "Listen, Mr. Krokow, was it? If you want to talk about the practice, you should schedule an appointment in the morning."

He tried to sound authoritarian, but he doubted if it was working.

"It's Krukov, Slavomir Krukov, Tripp. Now if I wanted to schedule an appointment with Tara or Michelle I would have. I want you to Google me. Don't worry, I'm not going anywhere."

This guy is fucking freaky. Jesus, I'm gonna die right here. Tripp, starting to sweat, leaned against the door hard and typed the guy's name into Google.

HOLY FUCK. How the hell is a Russian Oligarch at my goddamn door?

"Mr. Krukov, why the fuck is a Russian shipping CEO standing at my door very late at night?"

Krukov laughed. The fucking psychopath standing at Tripp's door chuckled.

"I suppose that is a good question. I do not like to draw attention to myself and want to get involved with your work."

"My work? I'm sorry I really don't understand how I could help you. If you want I can give you the office number and we can talk about it tomorrow," Tripp said in a last attempt to get them to leave. He might need to call the police.

Slavomir was getting tired of the bullshit. He was really starting to think that the violence option was looking better and better. He could see Alex fidgeting with his jacket. He wanted to get off the stoop quickly but knew better than to say anything.

"Tripp, have you ever wanted something so bad that you were willing to do anything to get it? If you'd permit me, I'll tell you face to face how I ended up on your steps."

As Slavomir was saying this, he signaled to his guards to get ready to enter anyways. Either way, he was getting what he wanted.

That last sentence struck Tripp. What would he do to get the CF trial funded?

Deciding to take the risk, Tripp unlocked the door and pulled it open. Still holding his vodka and ginger ale, he looked at the Russian and asked, "Want a drink?"

Slavomir smiled and said, "Please, vodka, neat, if you have it."

In Russian, Slavomir told Alex and Arkady to wait in the foyer. Following Tripp into the kitchen, Slavomir started, "You must have a lot of questions."

Handing him a glass filled with Grey Goose, Tripp said, "Yea, how do you know where I live? I almost called the police."

Tripp surveyed the man currently sipping straight vodka. The tall Russian was well built and kept his hair very short. He seemed very calm, almost too calm. He wasn't as scary as the guard dogs that he left in his foyer. Those guys looked lethal.

Slavomir took another sip of vodka before beginning. He preferred Ketel One but this wasn't bad. "I'm glad you didn't call the police. That would have been unfortunate (*I would have killed you,* he thought). I researched you Tripp. I don't like to go into business with someone I don't trust. Trust is how I got to where I am today. And I am here to make you the most powerful doctor in the world."

Tripp was taken aback. That was a very bold statement.

"How would you do that?" Tripp asked.

Slavomir ignored the question. "I would rather know if you can, in fact, edit the DNA of babies?"

This conversation was filled with weird turns. Tripp downed his vodka and ginger ale and made another.

Before Tripp could answer the question, Slavomir cut him off. "What is that you are drinking?"

"Uh, vodka and ginger ale," Tripp said.

Slavomir motioned for the ginger ale and poured a splash into his own cup. After taking a sip, he simply shrugged. "You were saying Tripp?"

"Well Mr. Krukov-"

"Please, call me Slavomir."

"Okay, well Slavomir, we aren't approved to do so in embryos. We can only cure adults. We don't even have pediatric clearance," Tripp said matter-of-factly. It was all public knowledge.

"I know this Tripp, but that is not what I am asking. I am asking if you can edit the DNA of babies or like you said, embryos?"

Tripp was getting nervous again. "Theoretically, yes we could."

Slavomir asked quickly, "Are you sure because you don't sound sure. You are losing my trust Tripp."

Tripp could hear a shuffle in the foyer. The guard dogs had moved.

"Yea, I'm sure. There would be extra steps but it could be done."

Slavomir sipped his now vodka and ginger ale. He had to admit, the ginger ale was a nice touch. He never drank soda, but he wanted to mimic Tripp. The man seemed very nervous. Rightfully so.

"Tripp, this is good news. So now that I know this, I have an offer for you," Slavomir said while casually sitting on a stool. He was making himself right at home.

"I trust you, and I trust you can keep things to yourself. So, here it is. I would like you to design a baby for my wife and I. In return, I would put you in contact with every powerful person in the world that wants a baby. A perfect baby. You would become more wealthy and powerful than you could have ever imagined. You'd be untouchable."

Tripp slumped back onto the counter. His thoughts ran rampant. *This is what all of this is about? Designer fucking babies!* He couldn't believe it. Designer babies were an ethical nightmare. They were a joke basically. No one in their right mind would even consider ...

It hit him.

"I'll do it, if you pay for my clinical trial. I'll make you a designer baby, if you foot the bill."

Slavomir didn't respond. He just sipped his vodka. He didn't like to negotiate. Counter offers were not generally allowed when Slavomir was at the table. He could kill him and move on to Dr. Stein but Slavomir thought he would need both of them in due time. He would also have to remind Arkady that when he asked for a brief, he wanted all the goddamn data.

"What clinical trial are you talking about Tripp? I've only heard of your sickle cell trial."

"I just started one for cystic fibrosis. It is the same thing as my sickle cell trial, just a different disease. I don't have the money and I need it by next month. If you pay for the trial, I will design you the baby of your fucking dreams," Tripp said, gaining confidence.

"How much?"

"Eight million over the next three years," Tripp said without batting an eye. He had done this to other investors no problem.

Slavomir's eyes on the other hand narrowed just slightly. Clinical trials are federally regulated and he did not want his name attached to the trial. That would be too risky.

"No. The FDA would know I was involved and I can't have that."

Shit. I didn't think of that. Of course, the guy who showed up at my door in the middle of the night would not want his name attached to a trial when he wanted a designer baby. He was stuck.

"Without that money, my only option is to publicly fundraise, and my whole firm would go down the drain. We could never raise enough money. I wouldn't be useful to you at that point," Tripp almost whispered.

Slavomir finished his drink and gently placed the glass on the island. "I want you to do that. Raise your money. I'll donate it anonymously through the public effort. It'll look like a benevolent donation. Who would you have to tell to make my child?"

"I would have to tell Dr. Stein; he would do the actual editing. I would handle the rest." Tripp had no idea how to get Morti on board with all of this.

Slavomir stood and spoke to Alex and Arkady over his shoulder. "Get the car. We are done."

They already knew that, but they complied with his orders.

Turning back to Tripp, Slavomir reached out and said, "You'll have your clinical trial Tripp. I'll call you in two weeks. I expect Dr. Stein to be on board and the public fundraising to have begun. Also, why do you want to do these trials?"

Tripp shook his hand. It was like putting his hand on a vice grip. "My brother died because of these diseases, specifically cystic fibrosis.

I wish he lived. Just to be clear, one baby, one trial. I don't want to make any other babies after this."

"You'll have your trial, Tripp. You'll have it," Salvomir said. He looked Tripp in the eyes and said one more thing before leaving. "I expect discretion Tripp, or there will be consequences." And just like that, the trio was gone.

Tripp pulled the tequila out of the fridge and poured himself a large glass.

"What did I just do?" he asked himself.

13 JUNE 2026

JACOB'S PICKLES

NEW YORK, NEW YORK

Morti did not like their new table. Ever since Aiden ordered that damn screwdriver, they had lost their corner table. Now they had to sit at a shared table where other people could also be privy to their conversations. Now they also had to wait until everyone was here before being seated. That was tragic.

Knowing he wouldn't be able to do anything about it, he went to the bar and asked for a cup of coffee. He added the requisite milk and one sugar and stared into his mug. CNN had reported the fundraising numbers: Eight million thirty thousand dollars in under a week. It was unheard of.

As the rest of the team filed in, Morti continued to wonder how they had done it. Generally, no one in their right mind publicly fundraised for a clinical trial. He could not come up with a single instance that it ever worked.

Once everyone was there, they waited an additional fifteen minutes before being seated.

Aiden, as usual, started the meeting. "It seems that we are in the clear for money."

"How much money did we raise exactly?" Tara asked. She had seen the news and couldn't believe it.

"Eight million, thirty-thousand, seven-hundred and forty-two dollars and fifty-six cents," Aiden said.

"Shit Aiden, that's a lot of money. Like a lot. You gonna run?" Michelle asked.

Aiden raised one eyebrow in response. "Needless to say, I am not going anywhere. All of that money is going to the lab and the trial. More importantly, it will be paying our salaries."

"Can we talk about the heat that we're getting?" Morti posited. It was more of a demand than a question.

"The FDA is quite angry. They've let Myers back in on the proceedings to determine if we leaked the information. They're also angry about the public fundraising that we have benefitted from but there is nothing they can really do about that," Aiden said.

"Fuck, they put Myers back in? Goddamnit I hate that guy," Tony said. He had taken the brunt of Myers's bullshit when the patient died from blood hemolysis.

"But what about the non-FDA scrutiny? I read about several organizations that are trying to set up protests and some conservative circles are applying government pressure," Morti asked again. The risk was much greater than he would have liked.

"I already have a news van outside my house," said Tripp. Morti noticed he was very quiet this morning. He also seemed to be on edge. He drank three cups of coffee just during the meeting.

"We can talk to the NYPD for some support. We can't do anything about the protests but we might want to call Cassie and Terry to make sure they are still on board. We want to make sure their privacy is kept secure."

Aiden was right, the Elms were the priority. Morti would need to talk to his wife about this. *She should move in with her sister uptown,* he thought.

"You all might want to take precautions when coming and going to work for now. Also, do not talk to anyone about what we are doing. Is that understood?" Aiden stared directly at Tony, Tara and Michelle.

They all mocked being offended.

The team took a break to order food. Aiden touched upon trial logistics and updated the whole team on how their Type B meeting with the FDA should go while they ate. It was an important week to say the least.

Aiden ended the meeting after he finished his eggs and let the trio go. Once they were out of earshot, he leaned in to Tripp and Morti and whispered, "Did we leak those documents?"

Tripp, who was still not interested in talking, swirled the last of his third cup of coffee and said, "I thought you didn't want to be clued in?"

Aiden shook his head and left.

"What's wrong with you?" Morti asked Tripp.

Tripp looked around the restaurant. The brick and wood felt cozy in the morning. June sun came in through the windows and people sat, lined up in little pairs, waiting for their delicious troughs of biscuits and gravy. He had run out of coffee when Aiden left but he kept fingering the tiny handle on the mug. *How could I do this to Morti?*

"Let's take a walk," ordered Tripp.

Morti was now nervous. The last time they took a walk, Tripp had told him about his brother's death and pitched looking at Orphan diseases. He didn't like seeing his friend uncomfortable. *Maybe it's his family again?* Morti thought.

They left the restaurant and started to walk downtown. Tripp and Morti walked in silence. The only noise coming from Morti's dress shoes hitting the pavement.

When they passed 79th Street, Tripp broke the silence.

"We didn't get the money through fundraising," Tripp blurted. The tension was killing him. Morti stopped walking and turned toward Tripp.

"What do you mean the money didn't come from fundraising Allen?" Morti only used Tripp's actual name when things got serious.

"A couple of weeks ago, we had no money. Our trial, the lab, us, we were finished. The only money we had was the money I contributed. But, this guy showed up at my house and offered us a deal," Tripp said while restarting the walk.

Morti grabbed his arm.

"Who the fuck was this guy Allen?"

"His name is Slavomir Krukov, he is a Russian Shipping CEO."

"What was the fucking deal?"

Tripp held his breath. "He'd funnel us the money, if we designed him a baby."

Morti turned away from Tripp. He started pacing. *What the actual fuck was he thinking?* "We could go to fucking jail Allen!" he yelled. He kicked a garbage can. He kicked it again. He kicked it again and again and again until he was out of breath.

"I know Morti, but what about Cassie?"

Morti stopped and glared at Tripp. "That's fucking low. Are you kidding me? What's next, throwing your brother into this? Cassie and Terry would be fine, if we didn't do this. I don't think you understand what JAIL is Allen."

"It's one baby Morti. One fucking baby and we're done. We get our trial, Cassie and Terry get their baby, the Russian is happy and we get to be the heroes."

"Allen, I do not give a flying fuck ABOUT BEING A HERO." Morti started walking again.

"Morti you have to help me. This guy could kill us."

Morti stopped again. "Kill us? What do you mean kill us? He'll kill you Allen, not me."

"Morti, just this once. Please, I'm begging you."

"How much did he give us Allen? How fucked are we?"

"Eight million."

"Fuck!"

Tripp had been following Morti all the way to 70th Street. Morti was now mumbling to himself, kicking every garbage can he could. At 69th, Morti finally stopped.

"Listen, I want to meet him. I need to make sure I'm not going to jail. If this goes South, it's on you, not me. And another thing, the next time you decide to fucking sell your soul and mine to the devil, FUCKING TELL ME FIRST."

"Thank you Morti, you're saving my life."

"Go fuck yourself Tripp, I'm saving mine."

NEW YORK, NEW YORK

Morti was furious. Furious is probably not the right word. If there was a word for beyond furious, he would use it. Pounding up the stone stairs to his house, Morti was glad his wife would not be home.

He struggled with the lock, his key was not cut properly and he struggled every day. After another minute of jingling, the door gave and Morti walked into his cozy house. Although there were too many flowers for his taste, he liked his home. He felt at peace here. His wife says it's due to the natural light. He believed it was due to the relative silence and the ice cream in the freezer but he wasn't going to argue that point.

He walked over to the den and sat in his favorite chair while simultaneously kicking off his loafers. "Oh fuck," he sighed aloud.

What am I going to do? My life isn't supposed to be a spy movie with Matt Fucking Damon. Who is going to play me? Idris Elba? No fucking way. How the hell am I going to explain this? Well let's cut the shit right there, I'm not explaining this to anybody. Absolutely nobody. I can't believe that lanky fuck got me involved with a Russian Oligarch and being the Chipotle for babies.

"Why didn't he tell me first?" slipped out of Morti's mouth while looking up at the ceiling. Chicken shit was the answer.

It's only one. Hopefully one. Who the fuck knows, I'll have to ask him, if I ever fucking talk to him again. I guess eight million is enough to grant you a baby. Why can't rich people just adopt?

"I turned out okay," slipped from Morti's lips as he got up to make himself a sandwich.

I can't believe I'm fucking considering this. Who the fuck am I?

"What other options do I have?"

Not help, help, not help, help, run, report him to the authorities, no that would end up going poorly. Besides, I would never report Tripp for anything. So we're back to run, not help or help.

Morti continued to mutter that to himself, staring at the ceiling.

Maybe I can help but know that I'm helping? When it comes down to it, of course, I'm going to help.

"You pathetic fuck."

Morti knew himself. He cared about his work too much and about Tripp. There was nothing he could do. Logically, he knew that, emotionally, he still wanted to put up a fight.

I'm screwed.

19 JUNE 2026

NEW YORK, NEW YORK

Morti had been popping Tums since he found out that his clinical trial was funded by an illegal baby editing trade. He had to come to peace with it, for his own intestinal sanity, but he didn't know how. Talking to Tripp was not an option. He was still furious with him.

While reviewing patient files, he mulled over the ideas that had been marinating in his head.

Putting some distance between me and this fiasco would be good. Double blinding the samples would probably be the easiest way. That way I have plausible deniability. Has there been any paper trail so far? I don't think so.

Morti paused for a moment and refocused on his paperwork. He got caught in his train of thought and almost made a mistake.

He popped another mint flavored Tums.

I have to do something about this, it's killing me. Actually killing me.

He knew that they were going to meet the Russians eventually, he just didn't know exactly when since he wasn't talking to Tripp.

"I can't believe I am going to do this."

His stomach took another turn.

"Fucking Tripp."

24 JUNE 2026

SILVER SPRING, MARYLAND

As they approached the brick and glass building that housed the FDA, Aiden told them all to silence their phones. No one needed Tony's DMX ringtone to go off in the middle of a Type B meeting.

Normally, a Type B meeting is used to discuss clinical trials before the IND is filed. It was good practice to approach the FDA as a student approaches a master. Tripp and Morti didn't subscribe to that approach, hence their meeting being AFTER they filed the IND.

Aiden found their approach confrontational. Before Aiden worked for the doctors, he was a clinical trial manager for a major pharmaceutical company in New Jersey. That position was hard but it had structure. If you followed the rules and had a good product, you did okay in the field. That's why Morti and Tripp had hired him. His track record and working relationship with the FDA were both excellent.

Now, ten years later, that wasn't necessarily the case. Aiden called in too many favors fighting for the last trial.

The team entered the building and went about checking in for their meeting. They were escorted up to the second floor and asked to wait in one of the conference rooms. "I hope this goes well," Tripp said hopefully.

"I sincerely doubt it will," Morti snapped. Morti was very unhappy with the whole situation and had no problem telling them during the car ride. The whole car ride.

Aiden and Tony prepared their documents while Tripp and Morti went over some notes. Aiden would do most of the talking, but everyone had to be prepared to answer questions. Tripp and Morti would handle science and overall vision questions while Tony handled physical procedure for editing. Aiden would handle everything else.

As they continued to prepare, Dennis Myers entered the conference room. He begged to be on their review committee. After the information was leaked, which Dennis believed was done on purpose, he approached his boss and asked to be transferred back from medical devices. He really hated medical devices.

Tripp hated Dennis but loved to make fun of him. "Denny! Long time no see! No hard feelings about the last trial right?"

"Dr. Galloway, Dr. Stein," Dennis said coldly. He hated being called Denny. It had plagued him through school as everyone who seemed to not like him called him Denny.

Dennis took a seat and just stared at the group before him. Mr. Kim refused to cover up his tattoos while Aiden hadn't even acknowledged him. Aiden just tapped on his iPhone.

The rest of the FDA review committee filed in and made their introductions. Although Dennis was not the lead reviewer, he decided when he woke up that morning that he would not be sitting on the sidelines. After a few run-of-the-mill questions about timelines and toxicity, Dennis chimed in. "So why did you decide to make your application public?"

No one moved on Tripp's side of the table. Aiden fielded the question, knowing that this line of question would be coming. "We had the same question for you actually. We were not prepared to field all of the publicity that we are now dealing with, both good and bad."

"Well financially you certainly have benefitted. What was the figure again, wait a second." Dennis flipped through his legal pad and said, "Ah, yes, eight million and thirty thousand dollars, all from anonymous donors."

"That was the good publicity. The bad publicity includes congressmen and senators disparaging our work," Aiden said matter-of-factly. He wasn't lying about that piece.

"I just seem to find it extraordinary that just days before your meeting with the FDA, information about your IND was 'leaked', I use that term loosely by the way, and you raise eight million dollars in less than a week."

"And I find it extraordinary that days before our meeting, which will ultimately decide the fate of our trials, our information was released, drawing public opinion into the proceedings, giving you, Mr. Myers, the opportunity to come back into our lives and impede our hard earned progress," Aiden retorted.

A reviewer chimed in, "Now we can't be throwing accusations. We are here to determine the status of your IND."

Dennis and Aiden both sat back in their chairs. The reviewer that broke up the first bout asked several questions for Tony. This got the meeting back on track. Tony began to talk about how animal studies would be conducted when Dennis chimed back in again.

"How are you going to address the issue of cross-contamination and hemolysis Mr. Kim?"

"The subjects will be assigned IDs and all of the associated equipment that will be used in the procedures will correspond with those IDs, such as containers."

"How will you control for human error though?" Dennis challenged. That was what the team had blamed the last death on.

"The technicians will only be working with one sample at a time and within the operating procedures, the IDs are cross-referenced five times."

Tony felt confident with his answers. He hadn't slept for weeks after the incident occurred and had made the proper adjustments. He just hoped that his mistake wouldn't haunt him now.

Dennis had already reviewed the corrections. He had to admit, they were as good as he would have done himself. He just wanted to see Tony squirm.

Continuing the meeting, everything else went as smooth as it could have gone. The reviewers seemed receptive and Dennis Myers seemed to become more and more belligerent.

As the meeting wound down, the reviewers broke to discuss their thoughts in private.

Aiden was hopeful. The only contentious parts they had deflected pretty well.

A full twenty minutes had gone by when they heard yelling come from the other room. The yelling continued for another five minutes and ended with a door being slammed. The reviewers came back into the room and seated themselves.

"We recommend that you proceed with your IND, our liaison will send you the notes from today's meeting ... Congratulations."

The team was elated; relieved and elated. They could finally begin phase I and II. Aiden noticed that Dennis was absent after the reviewers returned. He had to ask, "Where is Mr. Myers?"

"He was called away and sends his regards," the head reviewer snipped. Apparently, àMr. Myers did not like the decision the reviewers had made.

As they were leaving, Aiden bumped into an old colleague and dropped back to catch up. Tony, Tripp and Morti kept walking and when they hit the lobby, Dennis was waiting for them.

"How did you do it?" Dennis yelled. A short, scrawny man, Dennis barely came up to Tripp's chest.

"Do what Denny?" Tripp shot back. People in the lobby were looking at them.

"You bought off the reviewers you smug cretin. How did you get to them?"

"Have you ever thought Denny that maybe they really like that we are curing diseases? If you took a second to smell the roses Denny, maybe you would understand that."

"You're a bunch of money-hungry fools and I will never let you get this to market." Dennis turned a deep crimson and raised his voice to a squeak.

Tripp remained calm and leaned in to whisper. "Have you ever cared to think Denny, that maybe you don't have a choice. You lost Denny, suck it up."

When Tripp straightened his back, Dennis threw a poor attempt at a hook. Tripp took a step back, making Dennis miss wildly. Tony, taking the opportunity for what it was worth, stepped in and put his whole being behind a right hand cross, sending Dennis sprawling to the floor. *Damn that felt good,* thought Tony. Lobby security rushed Dennis and restrained him, not that he was much trouble.

Aiden, from the top of the escalator, yelled, "Tripp, what the fuck did you do?" Aiden thought their trial was over.

"He started it!" Tony replied.

"Oh thank Jesus," Aiden said a little too loudly. At least their trial was safe.

Tripp, breathing a little heavy from the adrenaline, felt his phone vibrating in his pocket.

IX

24 JUNE 2026

ST. PETERSBURG, RUSSIA

"TRIPP, HOW DID YOUR MEETING GO?" KRUKOV asked. He was at dinner with his wife Anna.

"It went well. One person left unhappy, but that was expected."

"Anything to concern myself with Dr. Tripp? You sound out of breath."

"Not at all. The unhappy person was a bit difficult to handle. My associate Dr. Stein is quite excited to meet you."

Dennis was being hauled away, yelling like a banshee.

"Yes, I expect him and myself will have to discuss some things in the future. I'm glad you are handling problems so easily. You might want to work on your cardio though Dr. Tripp."

"Yes indeed," Morti and Tony looked at Tripp while he was on the phone. Morti was burning a hole through Tripp's skull.

"Anna and I will have to schedule an appointment," Slavomir said.

He found that to be funny, he even let out a chuckle.

"I expect it will have to be discussed." Tripp was not amused.

"Oh come now Dr. Tripp, you have to see the, what is it? Oh yes, silver lining. I am now at your mercy while simultaneously you are at mine. It is a nice balance. Send my regards to Dr. Stein and tell him I will be in touch."

"I will but please make it at the office."

Slavomir gave the phone to Alex while hanging up the phone.

"How did it go?" Anna asked with some curiosity.

Slavomir had informed her of the progress. She found the doctors to be quite interesting.

"Everything is going well. We will have to visit the doctors soon. Arkady will schedule the appointment."

Arkady noted that he had a new task. He had to figure out how to meet the doctors and arrange a meeting with the Krukov's. He also knew that security would be paramount as Anna would be coming. Slavomir did not like to put her in the way of harm. It appeared that Arkady would be taking a scouting trip to Manhattan.

25 JUNE 2026

SILVER SPRING, MARYLAND

Two weeks, paid leave. Dennis also received a complimentary bruised jaw.

Dennis could not fathom the turn of events. Pacing his living room, he mumbled to himself.

"How the heck could this happen? All I did was disagree and question the candidates. I didn't do anything wrong!"

Dennis threw the remote control across the room. The batteries exploded from the remote and landed in his fish tank.

"Why does Dr. Galloway and his heathens get preferential treatment? It was the Food and Drug Administration for goodness sake! No one gets preferential treatment and these smart-alec fools walk in and get whatever they want! And what do I get? I get a suspension. I have never been suspended from anything! Ever!"

Dennis was fuming. He continued to pace his apartment, kicking furniture and throwing anything he could get his hands on.

"I have to do something."

At this point, Snowflake walked into the living room and let out a loud meow. Dennis turned to look at the cat. "What Snowflake? What do you want?"

The cat walked up to Dennis and started rubbing his leg. Dennis picked up the fat cat and pet him behind the ears. Feeling bad for directing his anger at his precious angel, he let out a few deep breaths.

"I'm sorry Snowflake for all my yelling. I just had a very bad day at work."

The cat meowed in response. It was almost like the cat knew Dennis was furious. He loved this cat with all his heart. It had been his compatriot since he moved to Maryland.

"Meow."

"You're so right Snowflake. I deserve a vacation. The FDA doesn't know what they are doing by suspending me. The whole place will crumble."

"Meow."

"Mexico does sound nice."

Dennis, moving to his computer with Snowflake in tow, vowed that the next time he saw Dr. Galloway or any one of those people, he was going to give them a real piece of his mind. But for now a trip was in order before he did something he might regret.

LUDLOW, MISSISSIPPI

Standing in the center of the gym, you heard the squeaks of plastic chairs and the gurgle of the coffee machine. The old high school championship banners hung still, the air thick with the Mississippi summer. Fifty, maybe forty, people sat in awe as a tiny woman walked in between the center aisle. Her pace and rhythm was hypnotic, entrancing the crowd.

You could clearly see that Monica Green loved giving speeches. She fed off the crowd and basked in their unadulterated glory. It was intoxicating. Mr. Thomas from the Republican Committee had just introduced her as the "Vaccine Queen". She quite liked the name, although the opposite was true. She knew nothing about vaccines. She went to school for marketing, not anything science related. She did not have a PhD in Virology.

What she did know though was how to woo an audience and post articles that people liked to read. She was damn good at it too. Her blog, PharmaPhails, had taken off once the Zika virus had become a problem back in 2016. She had connected the Zika virus to the TDAP vaccine and everyone loved it. She became famous overnight. Ever since that point, she had been traveling across the country, making paid appearances and giving talks about the dangers of vaccines. She had given her speech so many times before that she could do it in her sleep.

"Do you all know how much money Pharma companies make off of vaccines? Billions. Do you know how much money Pharma companies make off of our children? Billions. DO YOU KNOW how much money the Pharma companies are taking out of our pockets?"

The crowd cheered, "Billions."

Monica Green held the audience captive for thirty full minutes with facts and figures that were not backed up by any scientific publication. They were actually taken from other anti-vaccine advocates. She disavowed every theory that said you should vaccinate your children. She had the crowd on the edge of their seats. Monica knew though, to get a lot of support from the crowd for what she wanted next, she had to bring it all home. Make them feel the rage. She needed a martyr.

"Can anyone tell their story? Is anyone brave enough to stand and tell these fine people how they have been affected by the evils of big Pharma?" If no one answered she had a story lined up but it was more powerful if it came from the crowd.

Jodi-Ann held her breath. She hadn't blinked since Monica had started talking. The woman was speaking to her soul. She knew her pain and suffering almost as if she had experienced it with her. This woman understood. And now, that woman had asked the crowd to share. Would she? Could she? Patty, whom she had carpooled with, nudged her in the ribs. Jodi-Ann hesitated for another second, and then slowly inched her hand up over her head.

Monica, seeing the hand, said, "Yes, in the middle there, can you give us your name and then share with us."

"Hi Monica, um, my name is Jodi-Ann Kapp. My little boy Jimmy was a couple of years old when he was given the MMR vaccine. Before the vaccine, he was a happy kid, a little quiet I would say, but, um, a happy kid. After the MMR, he stopped talking. He has said about two words since that day and screamed a few times. That's it though. My daughter, Leila, we did not vaccinate her and she is a healthy little girl. She talks and laughs and sings with the best of 'em. It breaks my heart to see what I did to my little boy."

Jodi-Ann started to tear up. She had tried to keep her composure, but she couldn't. She started to cry.

Monica jumped on the opportunity. She walked over to Jodi, microphone in hand, and held her. Jodi cried while Monica spoke into the microphone, "Jodi, you are not to blame for your son's disease. We all know who is to blame. Who would that be?" Monica asked the crowd.

"Pharma."

"Say it again!"

"Pharma."

"That's right … Pharma. Pharma harmed Jimmy and no one but Jodi and her son have to suffer the consequences. Do you think this is right and just and holy?"

"No!"

Monica had them. Now she had to do what she had promised Mr. Thomas and simultaneously gain some followers.

"So what are we going to do about it? Two things. One, go to PharmaPhails.com and support the cause to ban vaccines from the great United States of America." This got cheers from the crowd. "Two, sign-up to help Mr. Thomas coordinate the effort here in Ludlow. Our efforts start at home and by helping Mr. Thomas combat vaccines here, you will be starting to change the tide for Pharma across the country!"

More applause and chants. Monica loved what she did and she got paid quite a bit to do it.

Monica stuck around after to chat with the crowd and sell/sign paraphernalia. She really hoped she sold out this time. As the crowd and questions dwindled, the woman named Jodi approached her.

"Monica?"

"Yes, Jodi, thank you so much for sharing your story, I think you inspired the crowd," Monica said kindly. The woman, after all, had been crying on her shoulder a mere ten minutes ago.

"Yes, well it felt good to share my story, if only to help people. Is there any way I can help out with your cause? It hits close to my heart."

Monica paused. She would normally send people who ask to her website or some local person like Mr. Thomas. Monica liked Jodi's story though. It could be useful.

"I actually think you could Jodi. Have you ever coordinated anything before? Or set up events?"

Jodi was quite active with Leila's class and the PTA. She also coordinated all of Jimmy's therapies. She answered affirmatively.

"That's great. I'd like to talk with Mr. Thomas about making you a rally and event coordinator. I think with some work, you could really bring some positive momentum to the campaign."

Jodi was beaming. She could finally do something about Jimmy instead of just cry. She agreed and walked over to Mr. Thomas with Monica. This was going to turn into something great.

X.

1 JULY 2026

LOWER WEST SIDE

NEW YORK, NEW YORK

ARKADY WAS HOT. IN FACT, HE WAS PRO-fusely sweating under his suit jacket. Across the street from Tripp and Stein's office, he was waiting until lunchtime when the office would be less busy to make his approach. He sat in a Starbucks, his back against the wall, sipping on his water.

Arkady hated New York. Everyone was too close to each other. Arkady needed a little breathing room to be comfortable, and apparently, a Starbucks in New York was not the place to find that space. A heavyset man, also sweating heavily, was on his iPhone watching puppy videos and sitting very close to Arkady's left. While on the right, an English couple was complaining about the tea. Arkady did not know what they were expecting; it was after all, a New York City Starbucks.

Looking at his watch, Arkady knew that he should get moving in about ten minutes. He shifted his weight, reassuring himself that his gun was still in his barebones back holster. He clicked his heel to his knife, which was firmly strapped to the inside of his left leg. Last, but not least, he checked his pockets to make sure everything was still in place. This ritual was done religiously by Arkady throughout the day. It all started during his Spetsnaz training, when accidentally he forgot his knife. His commander at the time made him hack at a tree with a toothbrush all day, telling him that it was his personal mission to fell that tree. Needless to say, he vowed to never again forget his belongings.

Ten minutes later, Arkady rose from his perch and walked to his destination.

Taking the elevator to the suite, Arkady noticed the opulence of the waiting area. Apparently, Slavomir had chosen well. Arkady's mission served two purposes. The first, obviously, was to secure a time for Slavomir, Anna and the doctors to meet. Secondly, was reconnaissance. Arkady and Alex did not like Slavomir going places without them conducting a security sweep.

Seeing no one at the front desk, which was what Arkady expected, he crept into the hallway. Slowly moving forward, he heard laughter from the room straight ahead. Arkady stopped before crossing large windows that appeared to look into a lab. This too was empty.

He continued on, passing a conference room until he found what he was looking for: Dr. Tripp, hunched over his desk, drinking a soda and eating, what appeared to be dumplings. Arkady moved quickly, stepping into the doctor's office and shutting the door before he could look up from his food.

"Hey! Can I help you?" The words were out of his mouth before he realized who had just burst into his office. It wasn't a burst technically, the door was open. Nevertheless, an intrusion.

Arkady didn't respond to the question. He saw the recognition come over the poor doctor's face.

"You should not leave the front unattended during lunch. It is poor operational security."

Tripp looked at the Russian behemoth. For fuck's sake, every Russian he seemed to meet was over six feet tall and massive.

"I guess so. How can I help you ... ?"

"Arkady."

"Yes, thank you, Arkady."

Arkady remained standing as the doctor offered him a chair. He had to be out of here before lunch was over. He was to not be seen by the other staff.

"I am here to arrange a time for Slavomir and his wife to meet with you and Dr. Stein. Get him and we will coordinate."

Tripp sensed that was not a question, but more of an order. Using the intercom, Tripp asked Morti to come down to his office.

A minute later, Morti stepped in to see a large man waiting for him.

"How can I help Dr. Galloway?" Morti said politely. He did not realize Tripp was seeing a patient.

"Morti, shut the door. This is Arkady, one of Slavomir's ... associates. The man I was telling you about."

"You mean the one that you agreed to help design a baby? Yea, I remember that."

Apparently Dr. Stein had some negative feelings toward the idea, thought Arkady. He would have to remember to tell Slavomir.

"Arkady is here to arrange a meeting time, preferably after everyone else goes home for the day," said Tripp.

"No, everyone must be gone for the day," rebutted Arkady. That was to be made clear.

"Also, Slavomir sends his thanks to you, Dr. Stein, for agreeing to help."

"I didn't have much of a choice," Morti said. It was true. It was either help or die.

Arkady ignored the sarcasm coming from Dr. Stein. He should slap him, but Slavomir said no violence unless it is necessary. It was getting close to necessary.

"Slavomir and Anna would like to meet September 1st; obviously, at night," Arkady stated.

Morti huffed and left. Tripp simply nodded his head.

Arkady waited for Dr. Stein to leave and stepped closer to Tripp. "Is he going to be an issue?"

"No, absolutely not. Morti is mad at me, not Slavomir and Anna."

"If he becomes a problem, I will be forced to handle him."

"Understood."

Arkady paused a moment longer than needed to make the doctor squirm. He then proceeded to slap him on the shoulder, almost knocking the doctor off his feet. Before the doctor could regain his footing, Arkady was gone and in the elevator.

15 AUGUST 2026

JACOB'S PICKLES

NEW YORK, NEW YORK

Cassie and Terry walked into the crowded restaurant. The couple had never been to Jacob's before and they thought it was a weird place to hold a meeting. The brick and wood surrounded the cramped, farm style tables. Men and women in plaid shirts took care of loud patrons while huge piles of food were slopped in front of hungry mouths.

Aiden had told them to mention his name when they got to the hostess stand. The hostess, hearing Aiden's name, changed her attitude from cheery to smug. "They are over by the bar," she said with an eye roll. Cassie and Terry looked at each and shrugged. The hostess called out Morti's name a little earlier and they all followed the hostess to the back.

While waiting for drinks, Cassie chatted with the team about their nights. Tara and Michelle were cackling over Tony's apparent attempt to pick up a woman the night before. Cassie caught the last sentence describing Tony's foray into dating. "I swear it was like watching the Hindenburg. That shit was going down in flames."

Cassie cracked up at that one. Tony, seeing Cassie laughing, turned a lovely shade of red. Tara and Michelle laughed even harder. Aiden, always prepared, asked what the two would be having to eat. They both ordered biscuits and gravy.

As they got settled, Tripp brought the meeting to order. "Good Morning everyone. Cassie and Terry, thank you for joining us this morning. As part of the team, we felt it was only right that you come to the official team meeting spot. I'm upset you didn't go with the coop platter but that's okay."

"Thank you for letting us sit in; we're excited to hear how everything is going."

"Of course, Aiden why don't you take us through?" Tripp said.

"Right now we are three months into toxicology studies. So we are making sure that switching the exon 4 mutation that you both carry won't hurt anyone. We are also showing that the transfusion process, which we used for sickle cell, is still not toxic. This also gives Tony and Dr. Stein time to perfect their technique before moving on to animal studies, or your own cells. We plan on having this done by late 2028, so we can get going with the actual important stuff, like trying to get you a baby."

"Why does it take so long?" Terry asked curiously. He couldn't believe that a couple of tests could take over two years.

"We want to make sure when we go to the FDA that we are going to be granted phase II/IIa studies. So, we make sure to repeat all of our tests and if we see anything that looks funny, we follow it all the way through. We are looking to cure people and that means we have to move slowly, unfortunately."

Satisfied, Terry sat back in his chair. Aiden continued to review the finer points of chemical analysis, which Terry did not pay attention to. He was more concerned about breakfast. He had gone for a run before the meeting and was quite hungry.

They paused the meeting to refill on refreshments. During the lull, Cassie asked, "How did the actual phase I meeting go anyways? I feel like one day we just got the green light and we were off and running."

Tripp fielded the question because Aiden's mouth was full. "It went really well. We had one reviewer who gave us a hard time, but we have dealt with him before. We knew it was coming. And yes, it kind of does go like that. We take a hands-on approach with the FDA so our meeting should have been a pre-IND meeting but we made it into a decision meeting. We will do the same thing for phase II and IIa."

Aiden, once he swallowed his coffee, responded, "I also heard from my colleagues at the FDA that the tough reviewer was removed from our cases. He was also suspended for two weeks due to his last outburst with us. So, we should be smooth sailing."

XI.

1 SEPTEMBER 2026

LOWER WEST SIDE

NEW YORK, NEW YORK

ALEX AND ARKADY WERE IN THE FRONT OF the Mercedes Maybach, while Slavomir and Anna were in the back. Slavomir was reviewing the data from the phase I trial so far. It seemed to be going well. Although unfamiliar to him, Slavomir could piece together, via the graphs and summaries, that they still had a long way to go but it looked positive. Positive, in this case, was very good for Slavomir and Anna.

"Do you want to read the report?" Slavomir asked Anna.

"Please."

Slavomir handed his beautiful wife the file and gave her a kiss. He was very excited about this meeting. More excited than he should let himself be. Anna skimmed the document. She had finished the summaries when Alex announced that they had arrived.

Arkady stepped out and opened the door for Anna and Slavomir after he had scanned the perimeter. The plan was for Arkady to escort the couple to the meeting while Alex stayed with the car and acted as backup. He would also survey the building for anyone else entering.

Although Arkady was paid to protect Slavomir, Anna was placed in the middle, between the two giant men. Slavomir had explicitly told his guards that if Anna was with them, she was the priority. He also warned that the consequences for them and their families would be severe if that rule wasn't followed.

Exiting the elevator, Dr. Tripp met them in the waiting room and introduced himself to Anna with a smile. She returned the gesture. Tripp had to admit, Anna was beautiful. In fact, he felt a pang of jealousy course through his stomach.

Tripp led them to the conference room where Morti was waiting. Arkady was left in the waiting room, guarding the door.

"Would you like anything to drink?" Tripp asked.

"No, let's get started. First, Dr. Stein, Dr. Tripp speaks very highly of you," Slavomir said through a smile.

Dr. Stein responded calmly. He was getting pretty tired of tall Russians. "Thank you Mr. Krukov, I have to admit, I am still hesitant with this whole situation. You have to realize the potential complications that are involved."

Slavomir was glad Dr. Stein was being polite around his wife. She had that effect on people. "I understand Dr. Stein. I assure you though that nothing bad will happen to you in terms of legal ramifications. As long as everything goes to plan, you will be very happy with the end result."

Tripp recognized the subtle threat and wondered if Morti heard it as well. If he did, Morti didn't let on. Morti continued on, "So tell us, why are you here today?"

Anna spoke up, "I am a carrier for hemophilia and Slavomir and I cannot risk having children that could die."

Both Morti and Tripp were surprised. They hadn't expected disease state modification, they were only thinking about cosmetic modifications. To top it all off, hemophilia was a X-linked recessive disease. Meaning they would have to edit sex chromosomes, something they had never done before.

"That complicates things," Morti said as a matter of fact. Morti seemed determined to drive this meeting, effectively putting Tripp in the passenger seat. Morti wasn't going to take this one sitting down apparently.

"Why?" Slavomir countered. He did not like complications. He reflexively leaned forward, preparing for a fight.

"Editing sex chromosomes, where the disease state is located, has never been done before by us."

"Can you do it, though?"

"I suppose. I am just forewarning you that it will be more complicated than I was originally told. Also, your kids could manage their hemophilia," Morti said while he glared at Tripp for an uncomfortable amount of time.

Anna and Slavomir both seemed relieved. They, just like any other couple that came into the office, wanted one thing, to walk out with a child.

Anna continued, "They could but we do not want them to have that burden. It's a non-starter for us. Can we talk about the rest of the editing? I am rather curious on how the process works."

Morti answered, "Absolutely. So I guess the next question is, what are you looking for?"

Slavomir and Anna looked at each other. This is the moment they had been discussing in private for months. They went back and forth on every detail. They had poured over papers to understand what they could select and what was still not possible.

Slavomir took the lead. "We would like to have a boy with light hair and green eyes, like myself. We want him to not have hemophilia. We would also like to limit his risk for heart disease as all of our parents died of some form or another."

"Am I missing anything?" Slavomir asked.

Anna responded in English, "We would also like to change some of the markers we both carry for macular degeneration. We think the combination could be bad. We took it upon ourselves to have our DNA … what is the term?"

"Sequenced," Morti said while grabbing the paperwork. The couple was prepared, he had to give them that.

After a few minutes of thorough review of the paperwork, Morti looked up. With an intense look, he leaned across the table and stared directly into the eyes of Slavomir and Anna. He seemed to be peering into their souls.

Slavomir was not thrilled with the tiny man. He had to say he liked his attitude when compared to Dr. Tripp. This man was stronger. Slavomir would not tolerate odd behavior, though, especially from his new doctor. "Can we help you Dr. Stein?"

"The green eyes could be a problem, or rather a statistical improbability," Morti said while still staring at Anna's eyes. Slavomir felt his anger brewing.

"Why would green eyes be a statistical improbability Dr. Stein?" Slavomir said coldly. Tripp tightened, Morti did not.

"I do not mean to insult your intelligence with this explanation, but I will risk it so that you understand. In a simple world, brown eyes are dominant to blue eyes. We each receive a brown or blue gene from our mother and father. If you have one brown gene, you automatically get brown. The only way you can get blue eyes is by having a blue gene from mom and dad."

Morti paused. Slavomir and Anna did not seem to be confused, so he continued.

"Unfortunately we do not live in a simple world. Other eye colors exist, such as your green. We like to think of the other colors as an in-between blue and brown. The dominance issues still exist though. If anyone, such as Anna, has brown eyes, it makes the likelihood of getting green eyes very low."

Slavomir and Anna both shook their heads. They understood what was being said.

"It would still be possible though?" Anna queried.

"Yes, but it would be very difficult to find the right egg and sperm combination to make it possible. On top of that, I would have to edit the embryonic genome, which is also quite difficult. I will try though. I will NOT guarantee, but I will try."

That seemed to satisfy Anna and Slavomir. Morti was not done though. "Besides the disease state and cosmetics, I have two questions. Has anyone explained the risks to you and do you think you may want more children?"

"No and Yes." Anna and Slavomir responded at the same time. They smiled at each other.

"How many kids and do you want them to have similar appearances, as in light hair and green eyes? I recommend the answer be yes to avoid scrutiny but it isn't my children."

Slavomir had concluded the same thing but held his tongue. He and Anna hadn't spoken about it.

"Yes, that would be fine and only one more, a girl," Anna said.

"Okay and now the risks. So what will happen is you both will return here. We extract eggs from Anna and Slavomir will donate his sperm. From there, I will create embryos from those samples. I will analyze them and pick the best ones. I will edit the genomes of both your boy and girl. We will freeze the girl down with backup embryos. From there, we will implant the male embryo. The risks at each stage include miscarriage, infection, bleeding, all of the risks associated with pregnancy and other risks including death and sterilization. I have to tell you, this is risky. And you will most likely need to be put on hormones to stabilize the pregnancy during the first trimester. Tripp will take over after I implant the embryo and he will act as your OB/GYN through birth. Although I am an OB, we thought it was prudent to have Tripp work with you in this case. The children will then need to come in for checkups as we have no long term data about spontaneous mutations. I urge you to consider everything before agreeing to the next steps."

Morti, above all else, was a professional. He wanted to make sure that the couple sitting before him, no matter how rich, dangerous or powerful, understood what they were getting themselves into.

XII.

11 APRIL 2027

NEW YORK, NEW YORK

THE OFFICE WAS EMPTY EXCEPT FOR THE
sound of Hozier coming from the lab. The music helped Morti stay
focused. A white lab coat over his sweater and slacks, he was staring at
the computer, reading data coming from some of the samples collected
from Slavomir and Anna. Morti felt pretty confident that they were
going to get exactly what they wanted.

"Those damn eyes though," Morti said out loud.

He was going to have to extract quite a few eggs from Anna in
order to find the right match for Slavomir's DNA. Green eyes were
going to be an issue. The odds of getting two embryos in a row that
will both end up with green eyes was approximately 1 in 10,000, if they
were doing this naturally. Not very good. He would just pick the two
embryos that were closest and make minor edits from there.

*I may get lucky though. It's really the expression strength that
may screw me. The brown eye genes are just so strong. Who the hell
knows these days. Also, casually, I've gone from one baby to two babies.
Ridiculous.*

He also thought it was interesting that he was now agreeing to two babies instead of the one. So now he has a 1 in 10,000 shot in making the Russians happy.

Morti re-read their sequencing data to make sure he highlighted the correct portions that he was considering editing. He needed to create a few more sequences for insertion but it wasn't going to be that big of a deal. He just needed the time to do it. Coming in on Sundays was aggravating to his wife but it was the only time he could work without Tony over his shoulder. He also didn't want to alarm Aiden. He felt awful, sneaking around and keeping secrets. It really wasn't in Morti's DNA. He wasn't made to be this dishonest.

As Morti continued to scan the reports, he continued to highlight areas that may be of concern. A minor gene for Alzheimers over here, take out the Macular Degeneration genes over there. Look to make sure all of the potential combinations between Slavomir and Anna look favorable.

"Not too bad," Morti said over Hozier crooning about Jackie and Wilson.

The next step in this process for Morti will be to try and create embryos with favorable outcomes that limit editing. In reality, he did not have much control over the sample production process as that was up to Slavomir and Anna. He could only work with what he was given. That would not stop him from having to do some very delicate sequencing to figure out which embryos to proceed with. He didn't want to waste his time but needed to be thorough, especially with Anna's samples. There were only so many eggs that could be harvested.

Once those samples were evaluated, he would pick the best embryos, one boy and one girl, and edit them accordingly. This way, they would be perfect.

They need to be perfect.

5 JUNE 2027

LOWER WEST SIDE

NEW YORK, NEW YORK

Dr. Stein was nervous. He had not stopped sweating since he had woken up this morning, so much so that his wife wanted him to stay home sick. If she only knew what the risks were if he actually stayed home that day.

He had Ivan and Igor, or whatever the fuck their names were, hovering behind the door that divided the procedure room. He had Mr. Krukov who kept pacing the room as he worked. The man needed a sedative desperately. As Dr. Stein inserted the completely edited embryo into Anna, Tripp worked to keep Slavomir calm. The man wanted to rip Dr. Stein's limbs from his body. Apparently, Slavomir did not trust Dr. Stein with his wife's uterus.

They had chosen today due to the lack of personnel that comes in over the weekend. The only person they had to worry about was Aiden, and he had a bachelorette party to go to for his sister in Atlantic City. It was the only opportunity they would probably have all summer to do an implantation without Aiden noticing. No one could match Aiden's ethic; he was a workhorse.

Months before Anna, Slavomir and the guards had returned to the office several times for egg/sperm extractions, editing updates and operational briefings. Morti had checked everything, from sperm motility to uterine lining thickness. These two were completely able to have a child together. The only thing holding them back was their genes. Luckily, Morti had no problem editing the X-chromosomes.

The only difficult moments for the baby design, as expected, were related to achieving green eyes in the embryos. Dr. Stein had trouble finding a combination of sperm and egg that would be able to provide enough 'oomph'. Trying to explain this to Slavomir and Anna in the pre-op meeting was difficult. Dr. Stein used 'oomph' to describe penetrance to parents who were not of the scientific realm. 'Oomph' refers to the amount of penetrating or breakthrough power a gene has, or in other terms, how strongly a gene is expressed. 'Oomph' does not translate well into Russian.

It took a few minutes but they eventually got there. Slavomir's striking green eyes were a result of an 'oomph' mismatch. His mother's blue eye genes were able to overpower his father's brown eyes to a certain extent. This mismatch, in combination with a favorable combination of other genes that influence eye color, gave him his green eyes.

Now Anna has very strong brown eye genes. This means that the combination of other eye genes in the embryos need to overcome a very large obstacle. Luckily, Dr. Stein was able to utilize the genes from Slavomir's mother and father to create a favorable outcome. The children may end up with hazel, but it will be close enough. Slavomir and Anna were not going to complain over Hazel.

"Everything else, besides the Hazel eyes, is going to be okay?" Anna asked for the fourth time.

"Yes, everything else will be fine. The embryos are sound, I just did not want you to be disappointed if they are not exactly a green-eyed match to Slavomir. They will be close but could be slightly off. Now let's get you prepped Anna."

While the couple was in the office and Anna was getting ready for her procedure, Tripp took the time to update Slavomir on the clinical trial. All of the proceedings had gone fairly smoothly up to this point.

Their efficacy studies, basically duplicated from the sickle cell trial, were going great. Aiden was over halfway done with the reports. The last steps were coming into place nicely. Those steps though would mostly take over a year. Research was a slow process, one that Tripp was beginning to hate.

It had been about thirty minutes since Morti started the procedure. He spent most of that time triple checking everything. This was not his normal, run of the mill, implantation. Morti was in the process of checking the depth of the implantation in the uterine lining for the last time when Slavomir finally lost it.

"Dr. Stein, are you finished yet? My patience is wearing very thin. This seems to be too long."

"I am checking to make sure everything is fine before I end the procedure Slavomir. I will be done in five minutes. Tripp, please escort Mr. Krukov out. I can't think with him pacing like that."

Tripp went to oblige, touching Slavomir's bicep, when the Russian whipped his arm up Tripp's shoulder and unleashed a quick kick to Tripp's knee, dropping him to the floor. Wrenching his head back, Slavomir whispered, "I am not going anywhere Dr. Stein, and you will finish now."

Dr. Stein calmly looked up from the ultrasound screen. "Mr. Krukov, I currently have a needle in your wife's uterus which I am guiding with an ultrasound machine. Now do you want to have a healthy and happy wife and child? Do you? Or am I wasting my goddamn time up in your wife's fucking vagina?"

Slavomir stood, hiding his anger under a blank stare. He should shoot the doctor right there. *Could I kill Dr. Tripp and Dr. Stein before he injures my wife? If I threw the scalpel on the table maybe. Anna would be very upset, if we didn't have this baby. Especially if the root cause was my temper.*

After a brief minute, Slavomir decided against the deaths and released Tripp. He proceeded to walk out of the procedure room.

Tripp let out a sigh of relief. He thought he was dead for a brief instant. Slavomir was fast for his size. *I didn't even have time to react before I was on the floor.* Tripp desperately needed a drink after that.

Morti, sufficiently riled from the incident, turned his attention back to the screen and the slightly sedated woman before him. "Tripp, get the fuck out and make sure he doesn't come back in here. Go fuck yourself for good measure."

XIII.

JODI WAS ECSTATIC. THE TURNOUT WAS BET-
ter than she had expected. Covered in fake blood, a microphone
in one hand and a clipboard in the other, Jodi felt good about this
rally. She had traveled overnight to get here on time. She couldn't let
Monica down.

In total, approximately a hundred people surrounded the wom-
en's health clinic. They were chanting, screaming and overall causing
quite a ruckus in the busy downtown area of Atlanta. Jodi was not
concerned though. They were on public property (the sidewalk) and
she had filed the appropriate paperwork. As long as the protestors
did not step foot on the premises of the building, no one could be
arrested. Running back and forth between the groups, she made sure
they had everything they needed. There were fake babies, fake blood,
microphones and picket signs. Jodi had thought of the idea to split
the group into two, thereby allowing the protesters to cover the back
and front doors.

Since Jodi decided to help Mr. Thomas, she had organized twenty-five rallies in six states across the South. She helped Monica write

blog posts and designed the newest t-shirts. Jodi was a protesting machine. In her mind, by taking on vaccines and abortions, she was helping her son reclaim the life he deserved. Jodi also recognized that it was much easier to recruit people by protesting abortions than by protesting vaccines. Monica had helped her see that.

The rally lasted for hours. Protesters screamed and taunted the women going into the clinic. Jodi had no sympathy. It could have been her son being killed in there.

As the taunting continued, one couple walked out of the back door, trying to get to their car. Jodi, spotting the couple, started taunting them. "How does it feel? How does it feel to know you just murdered an innocent child. You should be ashamed of the sins you've committed! There is always a place in hell for people who spill the blood of innocents!"

The couple seemed young, probably early twenties. The man helped the woman into the car and shut the door. He was a thick man, the type of man that worked outside his whole life. Draped in a plaid shirt and an Atlanta Braves hat, he quickly made a beeline for Jodi and started yelling.

"Do you know what you're doin'? Making people feel terrible all day long. We're just trying to have a healthy kid and you make us feel bad for comin' here," the man said.

The man wasn't here to terminate a pregnancy; he was here to try and have a healthy one.

Jodi was about to respond when a fake baby, covered in fake blood, was lobbed from the middle of the protesters and hit the man square in the face. The man stopped, caught off guard by an unidentified flying baby that assaulted his chin. Looking up, with a streak of fake blood across his face, he resembled a modern day warrior, now decorated for battle. This man, who was just trying to do his best to provide for his future child, pushed off the ground with all his might and barreled toward Jodi.

Jodi had no chance to react. Her eyes stretched wide as the man wrapped his arms around Jodi's head, letting momentum do the work. They both crashed in a heap, Jodi hearing a visible snap coming from her left arm. The man got off two giant punches before the rest of the protesters could react. A protester side-swiped the man, knocking him off Jodi. Three more piled on to restrain him. A woman in the crowd called the police while the four grown men tried to keep the man pinned.

Jodi was out of it. Her eye was already beginning to swell and her arm throbbed wildly. The world was spinning around her. As she tried to sit up, the only thought that crossed her mind was that she failed. This protest was going so swimmingly too. Now it would be nothing. Monica always said that the media would take violence and use it to try and halt their efforts. Jodi had let that happen.

Her sadness in failure started to transform into something more. She felt it, like the old chain on the garage light. It took a few tugs but then the light turned on. This new feeling, a mixture of anguish, rage and new understanding, revealed the path Jodi's life must take. She realized, in that moment, while trying to prop herself up against a tree, that her injuries were nothing. They were nothing. Nothing compared to the pains her son had to endure and nothing compared to the pains she was going to inflict upon the pharmaceutical industry.

Jodi, looking back in the coming weeks, would want to thank that man for sparking her journey.

18 SEPTEMBER 2027

NEW YORK, NEW YORK

Aiden couldn't figure it out. He was off by one whole surgery. He was never off by a whole surgery. Lying in bed, Aiden was reviewing the inventory reports for the firm. He was missing thousands of dollars' worth of inventory. He had checked the schedule, the booking times, the surgery reports, and the doctor's time reports. Everything appeared normal except for the inventory reports. You do not, all of a sudden, have an IVF kit walk out the door.

While pondering the discrepancy and trying to find a good explanation to give to the docs, last night's conquest walked out of the bathroom. The banker bro who didn't want to come out of the closet was drying off. He said what every other banker bro said, "Hey, so I normally don't do this; I hope we can keep this to ourselves."

Aiden had seen it all before. Jock comes to New York from whatever backwards state he was born in, takes a high-powered banking job with a bunch of schmucks, and subsequently trolls the lower east side looking for angelic men. Luckily for Aiden, he was angelic and liked people who looked like they had thrown hay bales all of their life.

"No problem hun, I've got some work to do; can you let yourself out? Thanks."

Banker bro seemed a little put off, and Aiden liked that. Banker Bros always tried to be in control. Aiden took that away from them. It was like crack to Aiden.

Refocusing on the inventory sheets after he heard the front door close, he wondered how the hell he had screwed up something so simple as an inventory report.

XIV.

AIDEN WAS THE LAST ONE TO THE MEETING. Tony was the first and made sure everyone knew.

"Hey look who decided to show up! Today must be opposite day, huh Aiden?"

"Shove it Tony I was working on something. Sorry I'm late guys."

Tripp and Morti didn't care. There was a month where Michelle didn't come to a single meeting due to a new boyfriend. He lived in Pennsylvania and she only got to see him on the weekends. Thank God the relationship was short because she wanted to start bringing him to the meetings. Tripp had decided that was not a good idea.

"Well what were you working on Aiden?" Morti asked.

"I found a discrepancy in the inventory reports. We are off by a whole kit."

Tripp didn't look up from his coffee but turned a slight shade of pink. Morti merely said, "That's odd."

"Yea, we are usually really good about inventory. Michelle, would you double check it for me on Monday. It is the IVF kits."

"Now that you mention it, we've been short on some other reagents in the editing lab," Tony said. Aiden could not comprehend how he was just hearing about it now. Tony was supposed to notify him of any discrepancies immediately.

Tripp turned another shade of red but continued to sip his coffee. Morti responded again, "I've been working on some things to expand our disease modification. Tony, I'll bring you up to speed this week. And Aiden, if we can't figure the kit thing out, don't worry about it. We should be focusing on the trial."

Both Aiden and Tony nodded. Crisis averted. Morti was getting very annoyed by Tripp's demeanor recently. He was a smooth talker until the smallest of problems arose, and then, suddenly, he was a pansy. No wonder Tripp didn't have a girlfriend.

He was actually a little concerned about that. The man was forty-five years old and had no prospects whatsoever. Tripp had mentioned in passing that his mother nagged him about grandchildren once a week. The man seemed to dedicate his life to the practice and from what Morti knew, that was about it. Well, that and caffeine. In the twentyish years that Morti knew Tripp, the doctor had one not-so-serious girlfriend. It couldn't be healthy for a man to live for work like Tripp did. Snapping out of his reverie, he decided he would try and bring it up soon. The man brought babies into the world for a living, you would think he would want one himself.

XV.

ANNA WAS HAVING TROUBLE WALKING, HER belly forcing her to waddle. She had to go to the bathroom, again. She went about every half hour. With all her heart, she hated being pregnant. It was terrible. The hormones, back pain, headaches and the smell of meat were horrible. Overall, she wanted to kill everyone around her.

Slavomir had thought about killing Anna twice. The first time, she threw up on his shoes in the morning, drenching his socks in last night's chocolate ice cream. The second time, she threw his hamburger out the window because of the smell. She was not a nice pregnant woman. Whoever said pregnant women glowed obviously was blind.

Both Alex and Arkady helped Anna out of the Mercedes. They had to get a larger vehicle because Anna could not get into the Maybach. Dr. Tripp had ordered Anna on bed rest since their last visit. This was supposed to be the final checkup before Anna's due date.

As they slowly made their way into the office, Slavomir thought about being a father. He had been doing it more and more, thinking of his legacy and the things he had done. They never bothered him until recently. Looking at his wife, even with her surly demeanor as of late, he couldn't help but wonder what type of parents they would be. Would he have to tone back the business? Would he allow his children to see the world he so often delves into? What schools would they go to? All of these questions had plagued him throughout the depths of the night.

The elevator stopped on the fifth floor and everyone emerged. Tripp was waiting patiently.

"Anna, you look great."

"Shut up Dr. Tripp, I look and feel terrible. Get this thing out of me."

"It will be over before you know it," said Tripp. His specialty was angry mothers-to-be.

Dr. Tripp helped Anna shuffle to the room with Slavomir in tow. Tripp noted that Slavomir seemed tired but didn't mention anything. His concern at the moment was the woman in front of him.

"Let's get you on the table Anna. I want to do our final ultrasound," Tripp said mildly.

Helping Anna, she huffed and puffed onto the table. Tripp checked Anna's vitals, noting again that her blood pressure was a little high.

"You've been following my bedrest order?" Tripp inquired.

"Yes I can barely move," Anna snapped. Tripp just continued as normal.

"Do you see these numbers, here and here? This is your blood pressure and both numbers are a bit high. I want to keep these as normal as possible, so please continue with the bedrest."

Tripp began the ultrasound, swooping the wand to the uterus. Luckily, everything appeared normal. The baby boy seemed large, if he had to guess, six pounds by this point. He would probably gain another pound or two before he was born.

"The little guy looks great Anna."

Slavomir and Anna both smiled. That was what any expecting parent wanted to hear.

"Now, I have a couple final questions I need to ask you both. I have rights at Mount Sinai and New York Presbyterian but I wanted to leave it up to you, which one do you prefer? Second, we're expecting a natural birth but if anything goes awry, I want to make sure we're okay with a c-section? Third, do you have a car seat for the baby in your car? You need one when you leave the hospital."

Anna responded angrily, "Yes we have a car seat, we're closer to New York Presbyterian and nothing better go wrong. Now where is your bathroom I have to pee."

Tripp and Slavomir helped Anna up after a quick wipe down from the ultrasound.

Slavomir told Alex, "Help her get to the bathroom," and he complied quickly. Alex had three shoes thrown at him in the last month by Anna. The woman was difficult.

Once Anna was out of earshot, Tripp turned to Slavomir, "I need to talk to you about something."

"What? Is the trial going bad?" Slavomir asked.

"No, no, everything is going great there. It's about our arrangement."

"What about it Dr. Tripp? Are you getting cold feet on me?"

"No, I just think I need to tell Aiden, my lab manager, about you. I can't go running off to deliver your baby without an explanation."

Slavomir had wondered when this would come up. He had a plan though. From the reports he had seen, Aiden was the real brains behind most of the business. Tripp and Dr. Stein saw the patients but Aiden kept the whole ship afloat. Slavomir wanted that for himself.

"I'm glad you mentioned that. I have a proposal for you. I want to bring Aiden onto my staff as my family's assistant. He would take over some of the duties Alex and Arkady perform for me while starting the designer baby business."

Tripp was startled. He had assumed this was a one-time deal. That's what they had agreed on. Now Slavomir was making this a thing.

"What baby business Slavomir? We agreed, one baby, one trial."

"Dr. Tripp, there is a huge market for this. I'm already getting two babies! You didn't actually think we could just let all of that money go to waste? We would split it in quarters. You, me, Dr. Stein and Aiden would each get a quarter."

"No, no way. I'm not doing this again."

Slavomir stepped forward. "Tripp, I could do this without you. In fact, all I really need is Dr. Stein and Aiden. I am being kind by letting you stay in the deal."

Before he could respond, Anna waddled back in with Alex.

"Dr. Tripp, are we through here?" Anna snipped.

"Yes Anna, you are free to go, just make sure you stay off your feet," Tripp replied. His head had begun to pound.

Slavomir turned toward Anna, but before he left the office, looked Tripp square in the eyes and said, "After the baby is born, all four of us are going to have a chat. Preferably, not at that awful restaurant you like."

Tripp heard the front door click shut and went to his office. Slumping in his chair, he grabbed a soda from the mini fridge.

Morti is going to kill me, if Slavomir doesn't. The only reason I did this was to keep the trial going, but now, he wants me to do it for other people! Morti will never go for it. Aiden doesn't even know about it.

Tripp was starting to hyperventilate.

What am I going to do? What are the options? The least favorable is a bullet in the head. I could do it, create a designer baby business and possibly go to jail. Or get another bullet from an unhappy customer. I could try and do it and Morti or Aiden could say no. From there, more bullets.

Tripp concluded that everything ended with a bullet to the head. The room started to spin. The sweat was crawling down the bridge of his nose. He grabbed his desk, trying to steady his breathing and apparent vertigo.

How the fuck am I going to get through this?

XVI.

7:30 A.M.

Fuck.

Tripp rolled to his left and placed his feet on the floor. His headache was at the forefront of his skull, greeting him like a surprise baseball bat to the face. Tripp made it a point to drink to excess the night before Valentine's, and then be too ill to go out on Valentine's Day. He hated the holiday with a passion. Ever since sixth grade, when Rebecca Hart scorned him in front of the entire class, he wanted nothing to do with the Hallmark Holiday. He usually took off and sat in bed all day, but Morti had begged him to switch.

So being the good friend that he was, or more likely, the single friend, he hopped into the shower and took a healthy dose of Tylenol. Tripp was also trying to get back into Morti's good graces. Last week, he told Morti of Slavomir's baby designing plan. Morti was furious. Absolutely livid. Morti, in fact, spent forty-five minutes lecturing Tripp on the ethical implications and legal ramifications of starting a black market, designer baby business.

In the end, Morti knew it was useless. They were stuck. Slavomir could either tank their business or kill them both. It did not mean though that Morti had to accept it lying down. He had refused to talk to Tripp until he realized he wanted to take Valentine's Day off. Even then, he sent him a text message that read, "I'm taking Monday, go fuck yourself."

So Morti didn't beg but Tripp took it as a fresh start.

8:30 A.M.

Scarfing down a buttered scone and his first cup of coffee of the day, Tripp left his apartment and hustled to the subway. He was a little nauseous and he knew the subway was not going to make it any better. This was prime time rush hour. He was going to have to stand like a sardine amongst all of the smelly people and he was definitely going to vomit. On top of that, he was going to be late, that was for sure. Aiden held a daily 9:00 a.m. huddle-up and hated when people were late to it.

9:05 A.M.

Tripp was sprinting up the subway stairs and turned the corner to go to the office when his phone buzzed six or seven times.

What the fuck? It's probably Aiden wondering where I am. This headache won't go away.

Tripp saw two voicemails and stopped to listen to them.

It was Slavomir screaming. "Dr. Tripp, when I fucking call you, pick up the fucking phone. Anna went into labor and Alex is getting the car now. Call me back."

Second message: "Tripp I am going to rip your balls off and feed them to my newborn fucking son. Arkady is going to be at your office any minute. You better be there."

Tripp started running and dialed Slavomir at the same time. His phone went to voicemail. "Slavomir, it's Tripp, I'll meet Arkady at the office and we will be at the hospital soon. I want you to be calm for Anna. It is all good."

Next he called Aiden. The phone rang three times before Aiden picked up.

"Tripp, where are you? Our first patient arrives at 9:45 today. You are 7 minutes late, the huddle is already done."

"Hey Aiden, cancel all of the appointments, my good friend went into labor and their OB is away on vacation. They called me in a panic."

"Tripp, we can't do that; we have a full schedule today."

"Just tell them that other patients went into labor and the doctor would do that same thing for them as well. I'm not coming in Aiden. Do not call Morti. He won't be able to bail you out either."

Tripp hung up the phone as Aiden tried to give a rebuttal. He really didn't have time. Tripp continued to jog to the office and as soon as he turned the corner, he saw Arkady standing outside the car, scanning the street.

Arkady spotted Tripp, got in the car and revved the engine. Tripp basically dove in the front seat as Arkady took off. He wasn't wasting much time.

"I guess Slavomir told you to hurry?" Tripp asked Arkady. The large Russian was driving too fast for downtown New York.

"If you didn't arrive in the next five minutes, Slavomir told me to go to your house, break down the door and drag you to the hospital."

"I'm glad you didn't do that."

"I think it could have been fun," Arkady said with a wry smile.

Tripp guessed that was the Russian version of a joke.

9:20 A.M.

Arkady stopped the Mercedes at the front door of the hospital. Tripp was about to throw up his buttered scone. Arkady drove on the sidewalk, the middle lines and almost barreled over an old lady and her Golden Doodle. He probably broke every law of the American driving system.

"Get out Dr. Tripp; you have a baby to deliver."

Tripp basically fell out of the car as Arkady pulled away.

Before peeling off to find parking, Arkady threw him a bottle of water.

"Drink this, you look like shit."

He walked through the front doors and made his way to the Labor and Delivery ward.

He knew he was in the right place when he heard Anna yelling in Russian while both Alex and Slavomir were pacing in the hallway.

Slavomir spotted Tripp and started bellowing. "Dr. Tripp, where the fuck have you been!"

The nurses looked shocked that not only was a man yelling at a doctor, but they were yelling at Dr. Galloway. "Slavomir, good morning, I was in the subway when you called. Thanks for the lift though. Now please stop yelling, so the nurses don't have to call security."

Slavomir looked at the nurses. They did seem a little startled. Slavomir spoke to Alex quickly, "Get Arkady and bring him back up here."

Alex merely nodded.

"Where is he going?" Tripp asked.

"To get Arkady," Slavomir said.

Tripp yelled over his shoulder, "He's looking for parking."

Tripp patted Slavomir on the shoulder, which Slavomir despised, and proceeded to go calm down the screaming Russian woman.

"Anna, good morning, how are you doing?" Tripp asked genuinely.

"If you ask me that again, I will slit your throat," Anna screamed.

Slavomir laughed and translated. Tripp saw why they loved each other so much.

"Okay well, duly noted. Anna, I have to check to see how everything is going. Can you prop your legs up for me?"

Anna obliged as another contraction rolled through. She yelled something in Russian again, but Slavomir didn't translate this time. Apparently, it wasn't directed at Tripp.

She still had a long way to go. She was only 2 centimeters dilated. "Anna, you still have some time before we can get started. How is the pain?"

"How do you think the pain is Dr. Tripp?" Anna yelled.

"Would you like an epidural? I can order one for you."

"Yes, now, do it now." Anna was moaning in agony.

"Okay Anna, I will order one, hang in there okay. I'll be back in a couple of hours to check on your progress. The anesthesiologist will come and give the epidural. Don't yell at them."

Tripp stepped out of the room with Slavomir. Tripp could see the giant Russian guards walking down the hallway, taking up the entire width. "Uncle Alex, Uncle Arkady, please come here."

Arkady and Alex obliged, understanding the implicit suggestion. Slavomir chuckled, all of the smoke and mirrors made him laugh.

"Anna will be here for a while. I would rotate, so you all can get some rest. Especially you Slavomir, you are going to have a long time without sleep once this baby is born."

Slavomir waved off the concern. "We don't need much sleep. You worry about Anna, and I expect you to check in more than every couple of hours."

9:35 A.M.

Aiden called in a panic. "Would you be able to cover for Tripp? He said he has an emergency delivery."

"Aiden, you know I took off today to be with my wife. You're lucky you called when she's in the shower. If Tripp isn't going to run his own damn business, then I am not cleaning up his mess. Reschedule everyone."

Morti was clearly not having it today.

"Come on, it's a full schedule." Aiden did not want to piss off forty people.

"Have the team take care of it." Morti hung up the phone.

Morti put his phone away and looked down into his cup of coffee. *The bastard couldn't even cover for one day. Anna must have gone into labor.*

The shower turned off. He promised his wife a full day of fun, starting with breakfast and the MoMA.

I don't know if I can keep doing all of this. It's wearing me down.

He looked up and into the mirror, inspecting the wrinkles coming from his temples. His wife thought it made him look distinguished. The wrinkles just reminded him of all the illegal shit he was doing.

I need to distance myself from this. If I am going to continue doing this, I can't be intimately involved. Maybe they can blind me to the samples? Getting Aiden involved could be helpful in that regard. I have to distance myself.

When Morti thought of himself as a doctor, he never thought he would end up being a criminal doctor. He knew doctors who did things discreetly for less than reputable people. He tried to keep his reputation out of that realm. The worst thing he would do is write an occasional script for his wife. Designing illegal babies for the rich and powerful? That was an unprecedented level of crime, even for the doctors who occasionally pulled bullets out of people in the middle of the night.

7:30 P.M.

"Do not push yet Anna, you need to wait!" Tripp said sternly. They were in between contractions and Anna could rip something. The last thing Tripp needed was Anna to bleed out on the table.

The nurses tried to fight having the "uncles" in the delivery room. Slavomir was demanding it. Tripp settled it by having Arkady step outside. The nurses were pissed but he didn't care. He just wanted Slavomir to remain calm.

Anna was plastered with sweat. She had shit herself about an hour ago. There was nothing anyone could really do about it. Most people were surprised that women tended to lose bowel control when giving birth. They after all were pushing pretty hard.

As a new contraction rolled in, Tripp tried to keep Anna calm. It was almost no use. The smell was pretty awful, so Tripp focused on breathing through his mouth. Slavomir held his wife's hand the entire time. Tripp thought he heard a finger pop earlier, but Slavomir never left. If he was in pain, he didn't show it.

"Okay Anna, big push now. Push!"

Anna screamed and pushed with all her might. The head was starting to peek through.

"One more Anna, one more right now, we need to get those shoulders through."

Anna gave it everything she had.

Tripp angled the baby to get one shoulder through. He was trying to avoid ripping the perineum. He hated having to stitch up mothers because he wasn't skilled enough to keep them in one piece. Luckily, today was not a bad day. The second shoulder went through and the baby basically fell out. Everything moved quickly after that. Tripp cleared the airways and pinched the baby pretty hard. The cord was cut and the baby wailed with Anna.

Anna delivered the placenta and finally let out a sigh of relief. The baby was cleaned by the nurses and wrapped up nice and tight. Anna and Slavomir couldn't believe it. The boy of their dream was real.

"The nurses are going to take care of you Anna. I'm going to get washed up and meet you in recovery after I finish my paperwork."

"Thank you Dr. Tripp, we owe you everything."

Tripp merely smiled behind his mask.

9:00 P.M.

After checking in with Aiden and filing all of the paperwork, Tripp made his way to Anna's recovery room. Anna was sleeping. Slavomir was holding the baby, quietly rocking the little boy.

"How is he doing?" Tripp asked.

"He is a strong little Ruskie," Slavomir said.

"I'm glad you and Anna are happy. He'll need to come into the office for some tests. Also, we can recommend some good pediatricians if you need one."

"Yes, yes we are. Thank you. We still have some unfinished business, but we'll leave that for another day."

Tripp had almost forgotten. "I still haven't told Aiden, and Morti is very upset about the whole arrangement."

"When we meet, I will settle everything. For now, let me enjoy my son."

"What's his name?"

"Leo. Leo Nikolai Krukov."

Tripp nodded and said good night. He would check on Anna in the morning.

XVII.

"THIS CAN'T BE A LEGITIMATE BUSINESS Slavomir!" Morti yelled. His volume made Alex shift a little. Everyone was on pins and needles since the conversation began. Tripp was basically in to save his own life and Slavomir was trying to convince Morti that his life was not worth saying no.

"Dr. Stein, I respect you. You brought my son into the world, but, you are trying my patience. I am not asking you to put a billboard up on the Empire State Building. All I am asking is for you to design a baby or two, discreetly, for very powerful people."

"Oh, just design a fucking baby or two. Slavomir, I could go to jail for life! Genetic editing is just now being accepted because the work Tripp and I do. If we got caught, we would set the scientific community back a hundred years. There would be riots. Can you imagine what poor people will think of what we would be doing? What we have done?"

Morti stood up and paced Tripp's living room. He was gripping his gin and tonic like his life depended on it.

Tripp piped up, "Morti, that's the thing; we won't get caught."

"How the flying fuck are we not going to get caught Tripp?" Morti shot back.

Slavomir, having had quite enough of Dr. Stein, said, "Dr. Stein, sit down now."

"No, I will not fucking-" Morti stopped talking. Slavomir pulled his pistol out from his back holster and pointed it lazily at Dr. Stein.

"Sit the fuck down Dr. Stein and I will explain how we will not be getting caught."

The doorbell rang. It was Aiden. Tripp went to get the door but Slavomir pointed the gun at him before he could fully stand.

"Everyone stay seated. Get the door." Slavomir ordered his team in Russian.

Arkady moved from his position near the fireplace to the foyer. Slavomir put his gun away.

"I would very much like the next part of this conversation to go well, so if you please, do not ruin it." Slavomir stated while staring at Dr. Stein. "And act fucking normal," he added.

Aiden was surprised when a very tall man opened the door to Tripp's apartment. "Oh, I'm sorry I must have the wrong place." *I thought it was this one but I only come here for the Christmas Parties, so I might have messed up.*

Turning to leave, Tripp yelled from the living room, "Aiden, you got it right, come on in, don't mind Arkady; he's the strong silent type."

Aiden was certainly confused but entered anyway. Aiden liked Tripp's place. It was clean and spacious. An open-floor concept with a fireplace and comfortable sofas. Aiden thought, he could live in a place like this one day, if he found a sugar daddy. *Maybe Tripp was taking applications? Or this guy, who is the mystery man built like a statue?* Aiden thought while looking at Slavomir.

Tripp offered Aiden a drink, which he accepted readily. "Aiden, I would like you to meet my friend Slavomir. He was the man who called me when we shut down the shop on Valentine's Day."

"Oh congratulations, you must be very excited to be a father."

"Yes, my wife and I are very happy, thanks to Dr. Tripp and Stein."

"Oh are you one of our clients? I thought you were just friends with Tripp," Aiden asked. He was usually pretty good with names due to the billing reports.

"Not exactly, please, take a seat. Tripp speaks very highly of you; I had to meet you in person."

"I have to say, I thought it was odd when Tripp invited me to his house. He was cryptic."

Tripp chimed in again, "Yea Aiden, sorry about all that. You see, Slavomir and his wife are private people and I needed to keep our interactions as quiet as possible."

"I see, but I am still confused what this is all about exactly," Aiden said. Slavomir could see the gears turning in the man's head.

Morti spoke up first. "Slavomir wants to poach you."

Both Aiden and Tripp looked startled, for different reasons though.

"I'm sorry Slavomir but I am very happy with Tripp and Morti and we are in the middle of a very important clinical trial," Aiden said.

Slavomir thought his loyalty was admirable, misplaced, but admirable.

"Let me lay it out for you Aiden, before you say no," Slavomir said. He waited for Aiden to nod before continuing.

"Tripp and Morti helped my wife and I have a baby. You see, Anna and I are from Russia where they are a bit, how do you say, close-minded about certain things. So we contacted Tripp and Morti.

Through our discussion, we discovered that we both had problems that a partnership could solve. Anna and I couldn't have a baby and your cystic fibrosis trial needed funding. So, we made a trade."

Aiden was floored. He looked at Tripp, Morti, and back at Tripp. "Are you saying that you gave us over eight million dollars for a baby? You do know that is way overpriced right?"

Slavomir laughed at that. He howled with laughter actually.

Aiden turned back to Morti, "Is this true?"

"Unfortunately yes, unbeknownst to me. Tripp struck the deal, and then informed me." Morti snipped. He was very perturbed at how the conversation was going. Slavomir had bastardized the whole sequence of events.

"Why?" Aiden asked Tripp.

"We were stuck and we needed the money. We were the only people that could help Slavomir and Anna."

"There are plenty of IVF specialists in the city. Why were Tripp and Stein the only ones who could help … " Aiden stopped mid-thought. "The baby is edited, isn't it?"

"Bingo, right answer!" Morti yelled, faking enthusiasm.

"Holy Shit." Aiden slumped back on the couch. *That is fucking crazy.* "I can't believe you guys did that. That's reckless," Aiden said, letting out a big breath. *They are most definitely going to jail.* "You guys know you are going to jail, right? Like not under Times Square on New Year's Eve jail, I'm talking Guantanamo Bay jail."

"I know," Morti said. He was pretty much resigned to that fact.

"No. We are all not going to jail. Please, Slavomir, tell them why," Tripp begged. He was getting too nervous for his own good.

Slavomir leaned forward. This was the point he was going to have to nail to bring Aiden on board. The alternative was a little … messy.

"Well, to begin, if we go down this road, we are all going to have to be unified in our decision. One person can ruin everything. So, is everyone at least interested in hearing the proposal?"

Slavomir stopped and looked around. Both Aiden and Tripp said nothing while Morti made a grand sweeping motion with his hand and said, "I'm all ears."

"Fine. So the new chairman of the science committee, Senator Chester Ashley IV, a very conservative Republican from your state of Arkansas, would like an edited baby."

"Holy shit," Aiden said.

"What does that mean?" Morti said.

Aiden hopped in, "Chester Ashley is the main opponent to anything related to gene editing. He was the senator that threatened to cut all of the FDA's funding, if they approved our trials. He has been lobbying against us from the beginning. Actually, lobbying is not strong enough. Railing would be more apt."

That was big news, even Morti had to admit.

"Why does he want an edited baby?" Morti queried.

Slavomir answered, "He has Y-chromosome infertility and would like to fix that in his boys. His wife and him have not been able to have children. I met him at a banquet and we got to talking. I said I might be able to help him."

"I don't know if we can cure that, it depends on how severe of a case he has," Morti stated. Y-chromosome infertility can be so severe that males do not produce sperm. It was caused by a deletion on the Y or male chromosome.

"That's why I said might," Slavomir said coldly. "What we would ask in return is him supporting the work that we are doing and back off all together. Call it 'a change of heart.'"

Aiden's mind was going faster than he could keep up with. Less pressure from the Senator would make his job much easier, that was for sure. They would need more though to make sure that they don't go to jail. "I don't know if that's enough to keep us out of jail."

"That's just the beginning. I met this man by accident. I know quite a few people, powerful people, who would be quite interested in your services. We would just have to figure out how we would provide those services," Slavomir said. He was feeling good about the conversation.

"I still want out," Morti said matter-of-factly.

"I'm in," said Tripp. He had made up his mind a long time ago but felt he needed to even the odds. "We can keep doing good with this money. More clinical trials, more diseases."

"Dr. Stein, there is no 'out'. You have already committed the crime for a lot of money. You really don't have a choice. So, you can either be willing to cooperate or we will drag you through the whole thing," Slavomir countered. He wasn't going to let Morti influence Aiden. "How about this, if Aiden is in, you are in. Hmm?"

Morti said nothing. He just merely turned his head to Aiden.

"How would it work exactly?" Aiden asked. He was on the fence about the whole thing.

Slavomir sensed this and decided being bold would be the appropriate gesture. "That's why you are here Aiden. See, they," he pointed at Tripp and Morti, "know the science. I know the people, but you, you know the business and the subtleties needed to make this work. You are the key to this whole thing. How do you think it would work?"

Aiden sat for a minute, mulling the problem over in his head. He sipped his drink and played with the ice, looking into the glass as if it had the answer. "I think we'd have to make them look like regular clients. Bring them in with appointments, make it seem like Tripp and Morti were the miracle doctors that all the celebrities went to. Like a better Dr. Oz."

"Okay and what else? How would we get paid?" Slavomir pushed. He wanted Aiden to find the thrill of power by himself.

"We would have to charge them twice I suppose. Once as a traditional practice for normal IVF. Make them look legitimate. It also gives them plausible deniability. But behind closed doors, we would have a barter system, I suppose. Cash."

"No, not just cash. Favors too. What type of favors though? Get creative here."

Slavomir saw Aiden getting excited.

"We could have our trials passed no problem. The cash amounts would be substantial because this is so dangerous," Aiden said.

"No, I want you to get creative Aiden. Ask for the impossible."

"I guess we could ask for anything really, depending on the person. Like a get out of jail free card from the Police Commissioner or something." Aiden had just recently paid a public intoxication ticket and was still a little annoyed at that.

"We'd be untouchable," Slavomir whispered. He was already untouchable. That type of power though, the ability to do no wrong, was intoxicating. In reality, it was what every person really wanted. Short-sighted people asked for money. Visionaries sought power.

"So, I would bring the people in. Referrals and personal connections only. They would do everything a normal patient would do but in the consultations, they would place their orders and Dr. Stein would do the editing himself." Slavomir paused but Dr. Stein said nothing. "Dr. Tripp would be their doctor, just like he was for me. We would agree on payment and they would get a baby."

Slavomir really liked the idea. Tripp was smirking uncontrollably. Aiden was still looking in his drink. Morti had his arms crossed, his face a mask.

"What do you think Aiden?" Slavomir asked.

"I don't think I could be your assistant. I would need to be in the office I think."

"No, we need to spread ourselves out, so there is less suspicion. We'd find a new manager for the office, so they would be unaware of what was going on," Slavomir said firmly. They might need a scapegoat. He also still wanted Aiden for himself. He was too valuable. "Besides, I need you to explain how everything is going to work to the clients. I do not know the science, you do."

Slavomir had a point. It made sense to spread out the working links, and Aiden did know the science.

Aiden looked up from his glass and at the people before him. What they were planning was unbelievable. They were going to make elite, perfect children. It felt wrong, Aiden couldn't deny that. He worked for Tripp and Morti because they did a lot of good. This wasn't what he signed up for.

But Aiden thought about the power, and the chance to be uncontrolled. He could do what he wanted, when he wanted. He could have anything. So far, he had worked for everything he had. He was damn proud of that too, but the chance to get to the next level, relatively easily, was intoxicating.

"How would we all get paid?" Aiden asked.

Slavomir knew he had him. "You would finish up this trial and start the next one. After that, you put in your two weeks' notice. You come work for my company, on the books, as my executive assistant. You get everything that comes with that. Dr. Tripp and Dr. Stein hire a new person. We split all money equally and all non-monetary things must be able to be accessed by all of us. So, we all get the police commissioner's phone number, for example." Slavomir sipped his drink. This was going well.

"I think that all sounds fair," Aiden announced.

"I can't believe you are going to do this. All of this is illegal!" Morti was fuming. He stood so abruptly, his drink splashed onto the wood floor.

"Like Slavomir said, you already did it Morti." Aiden stood as well. "I don't have what you guys have, okay? I have nothing. I would have to work for the rest of my goddamn life to have what you have, and now I have the chance to really make it in life. Don't I deserve that?"

"This is ILLEGAL, Aiden," Morti countered.

"That makes you a criminal Morti! Are you a criminal, huh? For giving that man a fucking baby? Cut the shit Morti; yeah it feels wrong but we aren't doing any harm. We're not killing anyone," Aiden yelled.

Morti stopped. *Am I a criminal?* he thought. Could Aiden be right? Was he as bad as everyone else? He was shaken, that was for damn sure.

"Listen Morti, I get it. Everything about this seems wrong. But the worst thing that can happen is we make some people very happy and get paid for it. How about you never meet the people? That way you can have deniability too," Aiden offered.

That was what Morti needed. He needed that measure of anonymity. Aiden found the missing link, and Slavomir couldn't believe he didn't think of it first. He was too focused on potentially killing the honorable Dr. Stein.

Morti let out a breath. He couldn't believe he was saying this. "Fine. I'll do it, but I don't want to meet anyone. Tripp does the consultations and the implantations. I just work with cells. Aiden, come up with a way to make sure the samples look like research lines. I also never want to speak with you, Slavomir, again."

At least I got what I wanted.

Morti got up and left, slamming the door behind him.

XVIII.

THE MERCEDES PULLED UP TO A GATED PLOT of land. Up on the hill, about a half mile away, stood a large home overlooking the rest of the territory.

"Good visibility and sight lines," Arkady said to no one in particular as he pushed the call button.

Tripp and Slavomir were in the back seat.

"Now, when we get in there, please don't fuck anything up. I will do the talking. Senator Ashley does not like you very much." Slavomir was correct about that. Senator Ashley, at least once a month, was on the morning talk shows railing the FDA, gene editing and whatever else he yelled about in his fifteen minute windows.

The gates began to move and the car made its way up the hill. It was a beautiful ranch. They could see a herd of cattle out in the distance. There was a BMW in front of the house, along with a larger pickup.

As they approached, Senator Ashley stepped out onto the porch. A short man, thickly muscled from a life of Ranching, wore jeans and a blazer. He was built like a barrel, a cowboy hat wearing, angry barrel.

Arkady parked the vehicle facing down the driveway and all three exited the vehicle.

"Get inside before anyone sees you. That's the last thing I need," Senator Ashley said sternly. He walked back up the steps, leaving the door open.

Slavomir, Arkady and Tripp followed the Senator, who led them into the kitchen.

"Let's make this quick. I have things to do today."

"So, Senator, we understand that you would like a baby," Slavomir said warmly.

"Yes, we discussed this, but the way you're talking about doing it is wrong."

"You believe it's wrong I understand, but how many times have you seen something done wrong yield a positive result. We're here to help Senator." Slavomir was laying it on thick.

"Bullshit. You want to trade. I may be shooting blanks Krukov but I'm no fool."

There was a tense moment. No one said anything.

"How many children do you want?" Tripp asked.

Slavomir cut in. "Apologies Senator, this is … "

"I know who he is. That's Dr. Perfect or some shit. The guy playing a god in the name of science."

Tripp turned a shade of red.

"The doctor asked you a question. How many?"

The Senator lowered his shoulders from his ears ever so slightly.

"I thought this was a one shot deal."

"Tripp, explain to Senator Ashley how it would work."

Tripp straightened. "Well Chester … "

"Don't call me fucking Chester."

"Excuse me, Senator Ashley, we could edit your sperm, if you are producing sperm, and combine it with your wife's eggs and make multiple children. In your case, we may have to edit your DNA so that you can produce sperm, but I would need to do more testing to find out."

"They can give you some live ammunition," Slavomir said, laughing to himself.

"What's the trade then?"

Slavomir, still chuckling at his joke, continued, "You get children and you have your committee reverse their position on gene editing. You stop berating us and allow our trials to continue, unimpeded. In fact, you are downright supportive. If we ever call again, you pick up the phone and make our problems go away. You make sure to support anything that has anything to do with us. That would be the deal. Oh and of course, if you tell anyone, we kill everyone."

Senator Ashley put both hands on the counter and looked down, thinking to himself. His hat was obscuring his face.

Two minutes went by where Tripp and Slavomir watched Senator Ashley tap his fingers, deep in thought. He finally looked up. "You need to back my reelection campaign this cycle. I'm going to get hammered for this. I need cash for social media campaigns."

"Done, but it won't come from me. Russian money is not good for United States political campaigns."

"No shit."

Senator Ashley came around from his kitchen island and shook all three men's hands.

When he got to Tripp, he stopped. "They better be fucking perfect. Two boys and a girl."

"We'll be in touch. You and your wife will need to schedule an appointment with me in New York," Tripp instructed.

"Get the fuck out." The Senator was less than enthused.

As they were leaving the ranch, Slavomir piped up. "I should have asked for one of those cows. It could have been good steaks."

"I think we got enough," Tripp said

"Speak for yourself, you don't have to pay for his fucking kids," Slavomir countered.

"How are you going to do that anyways?" Tripp asked.

"One of my shell companies located in the great state of Delaware will take care of it through our lobbyist connections. Some lobbyist somewhere will make a donation on behalf of the company. It happens all the time," Slavomir explained.

"They still allow that to happen?" Tripp thought that was a thing of the past.

"In America, anything is possible. It's the beautiful land of opportunity! How do you think all of these politicians get rich? It's not from representing the people," Slavomir said while scrolling through his phone.

XIX.

"DID YOU READ PARAGRAPH 2 ON PAGE 36?"
Aiden asked heatedly. They needed to have the paperwork in by noon. It was now 11:37 a.m.

"Yes, it's fine," Morti said calmly. He knew that anything Aiden put to paper was perfect.

"Are you sure? That's a key point for this whole CF trial. What about page 112, chart 3? Also, did Tripp finish reviewing his work? Where is that pile?" Aiden kept asking himself questions.

The reason Morti and Tripp brought Aiden to the firm was his track record. It was spotless. Every trial Aiden had worked on had passed. That feat alone was almost impossible. The only reason Aiden was undefeated against the FDA was his insane process.

It all began with Aiden commandeering Morti's office, which irked Morti wildly. Morti was a tidy person. Aiden's process was the opposite. The man printed out the entire report. Piles and piles of papers littered the floor and tables. He used seven different highlighters that he kept on a giant keyring to remind himself of corrections. He wrote elaborate flow charts on a white board and checked off points as they progressed through the milestones. A side note, Tony one time erased something on the board during the sickle cell trial. Aiden tackled Tony through the waiting room door, nearly putting three women into early labor.

The final step, which Aiden was currently doing, was reading through every piece of the report almost a dozen times. When he was happy with the report, Morti would send it electronically and order Aiden to clean up his office.

As the clock counted down, Aiden began to make peace with the report. He checked a couple more tables and read a few more key points. Last but not least, he checked the spelling of everyone's name on the report. This last task was a ritual Aiden developed at his previous post. It was his way of saying farewell and good luck to the paper child he had raised from conception. He was sending it off into the wild.

At 11:56 a.m., Aiden sat on top of a table, looked at Morti and said two words. "Do it."

On his order, Morti clicked the enter button, sending years of work off to the FDA.

Now this message was special. Not only did it send the Phase I trial for review but it also consecutively sent another message, a message asking to begin Phase II and IIa. This was the email that would officially put Cassie and Terry on the map. The first people to be genetically rid of cystic fibrosis markers.

Morti thought it was only right to include Cassie and Terry. He printed the email on card stock and handed it to Aiden. "Have this framed and sent to the Elms please," Morti said.

"We can't do that Morti; it's a breach of confidentiality with the FDA," Aiden said. He was a stickler when it came to his trials.

Morti let out a sigh. He was fed up with people cherry picking the rules they wanted to follow. "In all honestly Aiden, with what we are doing, does it really fucking matter? They're going to want it."

Aiden merely shrugged his shoulders and took the paper. He supposed Morti was right. What did it matter?

15 NOVEMBER 2028

WASHINGTON, D.C.

Senator Chester Ashley (R-Ar) did not like the position he was in. Not at all. He was the new chairman for the committee on Space, Science and Technology. It was his job to keep the scientists in check and the budgets balanced. His thoughts could change the pace of scientific regulation around the world. And within six months, someone had already reversed his opinion.

It was a blow to his ego, to have bent to someone's will so quickly. Chester thought of himself as a noble man, one with a strong backbone. He was ashamed that he was changing his opinion just to gain personally.

Walking out of his Senate hearing, Chester put his speech back in his jacket pocket. He would have to shred it in his office. On his short walk, he thought about the uncanny turn of events. He was finally giving his wife the only thing she wanted: a baby.

To put it bluntly, every doctor under the sun told him that he was shooting blanks. His wife had been devastated. But now everything has changed. It was his wife actually, who put him in this position. She was fawning over pictures of a new born baby when the question arose if she had children of her own. That question killed her every time. She had said no, that they couldn't conceive.

A tiny hope emerged when the man she was speaking with said they had a similar problem. He mentioned a doctor had helped them conceive when everyone else told them it was impossible. Senator Ashley's wife begged Chester to speak with the man. If only he knew what the price would entail.

Slavomir Krukov struck a hard bargain. The Senator would have to support editing the genomes of humans to cure disease, a stance he abhorred since the moment it crossed his desk. He would also have to have his own sperm edited, in addition to his new child's DNA. It was wrong, plain and simple. He would have had the bastard arrested, if his wife hadn't looked at him with tears of joy rushing down her face. She had received her miracle. How could he take that away from her?

Shutting his office door, he loosened his tie and took off his jacket. Casually, he tossed his speech onto his desk and poured himself a drink. He needed one after the flip-flopping he had just done, much to the dismay of his fellow committee members. While sitting in his chair, stiff beverage in hand, he reread his speech before throwing it in the shredder.

Chester Ashley IV
United States Senator, Arkansas

Members of the Space, Science and Technology committee, good morning. I have asked to speak on our first point of the morning, the regulation of editing human genes for therapeutic purposes. As you are all aware, since our initial conversations, I have strongly opposed the editing of human DNA.

This was until I met a little boy at the grocery store back in my home state of Arkansas. He was rowdy, as boys can be, talking to his mother about fruit and what was for dinner. I had mentioned to the mother that it must be tough having a boy that active. She smiled and said she wouldn't have it any other way. She said her son wasn't like this until recently, when he was cured of sickle cell anemia. At this point I had introduced myself and asked if she could give me some more details. Her nine-year-old boy was one of the first cured by Dr. Allen Galloway and Dr. Mortimer Stein in Manhattan. They had changed his life through their work.

The work I had been trying to halt was something abstract, and quite frankly, something I felt was wrong. This boy, asking if a banana is a berry, changed my mind. He made the editing of human DNA real for me, tangible, in a way. I am thereby altering my opinion on editing human genes for therapeutic uses. I hereby support the unencumbered use of gene editing for therapeutic use only and would like to propose an investigation into legislation for this topic. At this time, I would like to open the discussion to the rest of the committee for their opinions.

It was all bullshit. The whole story: bullshit. Chester knew that. He wrote it. The deed was done. Regardless, Chester and his wife had an appointment scheduled with Dr. Allen Galloway for January.

XX.

Charlotte Briston

to Aiden McDonald

Mr. McDonald,

I am writing to inform you of the statuses for NCT80974178X, NCT23954152X and NCT90634125X, the phase I, II and IIa trials that have been opened with the Food and Drug Administration.

We are pleased to inform you that NCT80974178X is approved. Please see the notes attached in order to proceed. In regards to NCT23954152X and NCT90634125X, we ask that you schedule a Type B meeting in order to discuss the trials.

We also ask that in subsequent correspondence, communication for each individual trial be separate from one another. This is a common practice that ensures the minimization of confusion. If you have any further questions, please contact me at the email below.

Sincerely,

Charlotte Briston

FDA Liaison

6 JANUARY 2029

LOWER WEST SIDE

NEW YORK, NEW YORK

The snowy day in January was messing up everyone's schedule. Aiden was almost beside himself as the minutes ticked by. They were currently waiting for Morti, the Elms and the new guy. Morti had been called away in the morning to the hospital. The Elms and the new guy were having train trouble. NJ Transit was not the best during inclement weather.

Tripp, Tara, Michelle and Tony did not seem to mind though. They sat in the office conference room, talking about New Year's Eve and their hangovers. Tony jabbed at Tripp that he, once again, could not land a midnight kiss while Tara and Michelle seemed to kiss everyone in Manhattan. The four chirped back and forth, trading insults while Aiden continued to ponder his own thoughts.

Did I make the right choice, going with Slavomir? I really like it here. The money though ... That Senator is already paying through the nose. I was actually able to pay my rent on time. But what am I even going to be doing? Probably, coffee bitch. A really well paid coffee bitch.

As Aiden kept thinking about his future and his massive to-do list, the missing pieces to the meeting arrived.

"Ah, I see you all have met! Everyone, this is the new Clinical Trials Manager that's going to be helping out Aiden, Jim Louth," Tripp said.

Introductions were made while Tara and Michelle ogled the newcomer. He was tall, with a well-kept beard and burly physique.

He wore a plaid shirt with a tie and slacks, adding to the well-dressed lumberjack vibe.

"Hi everyone, sorry I'm late, the trains are terrible right now," Jim said humbly. It wasn't good to be late to your first meeting with the company ever.

"Don't worry about it, we are late too!" Cassie said a little too quickly. Terry gave her the side eye. It seemed that everyone was interested in the newest addition.

"What happened to Jacob's? I'm starving." Tony had been grumbling about the lack of food since he stomped in.

"We had to deviate from our normal venue in order to hear Cassie and Terry clearly," Aiden stated firmly. He really did not want to hear Tony complain all morning.

It made sense, if Tony would only think about it. Their next FDA meeting was on Monday and the key witnesses for their very risky Proof of Concept trial had not been prepped. They could not do that while yelling over the morning brunch crowd.

Interjecting from the corner, Morti chimed in. "Right, so let's get started, so we are not snowed in until Monday."

He had been trudging from the hospital to the office all morning. He was called in due to four pregnant women falling in the snow. Needless to say, Morti was irked.

"Of course, Morti. So, as Tripp said, Jim will be helping me out with the Phase II/IIa and eventually Phase III trials for CF. I can't do it by myself. We will also probably be bringing on a business manager, so that way I can play a more traditional role. I'd like to do that sooner, rather than later, but we will see. Also, we are here instead of our usual spot because Cassie and Terry need to feel comfortable talking to the FDA. So, what we are going to do is run through some questions that

Jim and I came up with. Jim and I will try to push you, Cassie and Terry, but stand firm in your answers. Don't worry, nothing bad will happen; we are just making sure you are prepared."

Cassie and Terry nodded. Aiden had told them all of this when they scheduled the meeting. Cassie was used to presentations as a consultant. She was a pro. Terry was not. He loathed public speaking.

Cassie told him to just think of it as a conversation. The couple actually got into a fight over it. The fight ended when Terry pointed out that this particular 'conversation' could cost them a baby. The stress levels for both of them were through the roof. They were so close and having it all taken away would crush them.

"Are you guys ready?" Jim said.

The preparation took about two hours. Most of that time was spent on Terry. Aiden could see that he might be a problem. He was very uncomfortable with even the simplest of questions. They had spoken at this table before, numerous times. As soon as Aiden made the conversation formal, everything went to shit. He had to do something. Everyone was frustrated. Terry could not even tell them why he wanted a baby. He kept stuttering. It made no sense.

"Terry, I want you to say that you're nervous as soon as they ask you a question," Aiden said while rubbing his eyes. The man was losing his patience with Terry's performance anxiety.

"What?" Terry asked. That didn't sound like a good idea.

"No, I'm serious. Even if they ask you if you want a coffee, I want you to say the words, 'I'm nervous,' out loud. By acknowledging that you are nervous, the review committee will most likely start off slow, giving you the chance to get comfortable. We need you to be okay with questions or it looks like we're hiding something. So, I want you take a deep breath, say that you are shakin' in your boots, and relax."

It seemed to work. Jim continued with the questioning. By the end of the third hour, everyone felt a lot better about the material. Tony even found some informational gaps that needed to be filled. The preparation turned out to not be a total clusterfuck.

"Should we go over funding?" Jim asked. It was a valid question, but Aiden didn't think the Elms needed to know.

"Let's wait until later. Terry and Cassie don't need all that data."

Aiden wrapped up the preparation with the Elms and escorted them out. Cassie had done really well. More like spectacular. Terry improved but Aiden was worried he would regress over the weekend. The last thing that the team needed was their Proof of Concept to have a mental breakdown *at* the FDA.

Aiden was talking as soon as he was in the conference room. "I think that's as good as it is going to get. We can't make Terry any better."

They all nodded in agreement. "That boy needs to chill out," came from Michelle, who now was eating a sandwich from the fridge.

"What else do you have?" Morti asked. He wanted to go home.

"I just need to explain Myers's involvement in our trials and the Bristol Myers-Squibb partnership ... " Aiden was cut off by Tara.

"Waaaaiiiit, isn't that Myers guy the one who is banned from all of our shit? Who let him back on?"

"Yes he is that guy, and yes he has been cut out completely. I just have a feeling something is going to go wrong. So, if anyone sees him, do NOT speak to him. Just ignore him. As for the BMS deal, they get a cut for paying for the trial. I've been working on that for Phase III, so it doesn't really impact Cassie and Terry. They're marketing department and clinical trial network are way larger and better than ours. So, we thought it was worth it. They help us fund and we license our editing platform to them. Also, J&J was clearly out of the picture."

Aiden was running on autopilot. He had too many things to do.

Tony, finally perked up after the three hour torture session, spoke up, scaring Aiden in the process.

"I don't know about you but I am hungry."

8 JANUARY 2029

THE FOOD AND DRUG ADMINISTRATION

SILVER SPRING, MARYLAND

It wasn't just Terry that was nervous as they all pulled into the FDA parking lot. The building looked particularly foreboding in the snow and dim of the morning. It wasn't one of those beautiful snow days where the sun reflects off the drifts, warming your face. It was cloudy and wet, as if the melted slush wanted to soak your socks. Tripp felt a chill go down his spine as he hopped out of the car.

The whole team was here for the meeting, despite Aiden's arguments against it. Tara and Michelle had never been to a Type B meeting and asked to go. Aiden didn't think it was necessary. Tripp disagreed. The endeavor was a team effort and they had a right to be there. Aiden, seeing that an argument was futile, relented on the condition of their silence.

Morti held the door as the rest of the team made their way to the check-in desk. Terry and Cassie, fingers interlaced, looked around in curious wonder. Correction. Cassie looked around in curious wonder as Terry looked as if he might be sick.

Terry had spent the previous forty-eight hours practicing every line and memorizing every fact. He even went on the FDA website and memorized their history. Any normal individual would have been prepared, but not Terry. He felt like he had forgotten everything in the car ride down.

"How are you not nervous?" Terry asked Cassie, looking for any morsel of support.

Aiden jumped in. "We're all nervous Terry. This is big. But, we can't get caught up in our nerves. There is too much at stake. Just breathe and remember what I told you."

"I'm shitting my pants," Terry said in all seriousness.

"Atta boy," Aiden said with a pat on the shoulder. He couldn't tell if Terry was going to actually shit himself, but he took the phrase metaphorically.

The security guard told them where to go after giving them visitors' passes. They moved through the brick and glass building toward a conference room. It was quite similar to their last meeting, where they were left to their own devices to prepare.

After about twenty minutes, the reviewers trickled in one by one, introducing themselves as they went. Aiden recognized them from their last meeting. As promised, Myers was nowhere to be found. Aiden had called the main reviewer to confirm Myers's absence at the meeting. The head reviewer assured Aiden that Mr. Myers was not even informed of their meeting. His tone suggested that the committee was still quite unhappy on the turn of events from that day.

The last reviewer trudged in, coffee cup in hand, and found the last seat. As soon as he was settled, the meeting began.

"First, we would all like to congratulate you on the success of your first trial. We only found minor observations of which you were notified of, correct?" the man in the center asked.

"Yes we were and we are actively modifying those observations currently. You should have them within thirty days," Aiden said. Jim's job for the next week was to make the appropriate corrections. Observations are basically edits that the FDA wants you to change. *It was nice to not have to do all of the work*, Aiden thought.

"Great, now we have no problem with your Phase II study. Our main concern is with Phase IIa."

Aiden knew it was coming. "We would certainly like to address your concerns, sir. Please, how can we help?"

"We, quite frankly, don't see the rewards in this venture. You can accomplish the same results in animals. We think the risk is unnecessary," the main reviewer said.

The bastard has a point, Aiden thought. The risks were too great. He obviously wasn't going to say that though.

"We understand your concern, sir, and at some points we would agree with you. With that being said, editing the patients would allow us to look at continuity throughout their lifetimes, a process we feel would be beneficial before moving to phase III. Secondly, we have shown already that we can edit the genomes with sickle cell. We are looking to prove not that the technique works, but that the technique works for this particular disease in humans. Animal studies in phase II would be done at the same time but the animal studies would be more for safety of procedure and less for the disease state. For IIa, we specifically want to do this in carriers and not affected patients because we don't have to worry about disease state complications. Our third reason is we can look at embryology, as the patients we will be using in our IIa trial are married."

Boom! Didn't see that one coming. The look on his face when embryology was mentioned could be akin to seeing a car accident.

"Embryology? Are you planning to edit the embryos Dr. Galloway?" a woman at the end of the table asked. She did not seem thrilled with the idea.

"Absolutely not. We are looking to make sure the edits are continued through the male genome. This way, the patients would be able to have a child without editing the embryo. The child may still be a carrier, but that could be avoided through normal IVF treatments." Tripp did not want the FDA to think they were jumping ahead. It was better for them to think it may be a possibility, not a definite outcome.

"And wouldn't you want disease state complications? In order to see if this change would work to eliminate CF?" another man asked.

"Normally, yes, but CF has minor variants as well, and we would like to confirm that the major variant can be eliminated in non-affected before moving on to not only affected but minor variant affected," Morti said.

The questions went on for over an hour. The flow of the meeting quickened with every volley of questions. They had already come to two standstills over differences of opinion, not only between the two parties but within the FDA's camp. Phase IIa was becoming an issue.

"Would it be possible to take a short intermission?" Aiden asked. He was sweating and needed some water.

"I think that would be wise. After, we would like to speak with the patients though," the head reviewer stated. He too was sweating.

Everyone stood from their chairs. The reviewers left the room, checking emails and rushing to the bathroom. The team huddled together with a pitcher of water, doling out servings to those in need.

"What do you think? So far so good?" Terry asked nervously. Both Cassie and Terry seemed confused at certain points throughout the meeting. There was no way they were going to ask questions though.

"I think we're aight," Tony said unhelpfully.

Aiden looked a little beat up. Tripp and Morti both glistened.

"So I don't think we have them convinced completely about the IIa trial. We haven't balanced out the risks yet. We expected that. Your part is going to be important. Don't worry about it though; we still haven't even gone over procedure yet, which may dull their fears too," Aiden said hopefully. It was pretty much a toss-up for Aiden at this point.

"I feel like I am going to throw up," Terry said while turning an off-shade of green. Cassie rubbed his back.

"It's going to be okay babe; just hold my hand and maybe I'll get most of the questions."

"Here, drink some water." Morti handed him a cup.

Terry sipped and took deep breaths. Cassie had never seen Terry this nervous. Usually, Cassie was the nervous one. She had known that he did not like public speaking, but did not know the issue was this extreme.

Ten minutes later, as Terry continued to sip, the reviewers came back from the break. Returning to their original seats, the head reviewer began immediately.

"Your names are ... Cassie and Terry Elm, correct?"

"I'm really fucking nervous sir," Terry blurted unexpectedly. Cassie immediately whacked his shoulder.

The reviewer was taken aback at the language while one or two other review members couldn't stifle their giggles. Aiden smirked. It was the first time they had ever heard someone curse in this type of meeting before.

"I understand Mr. Elm, we have been going at quite a quick pace today. I assure you, there is no need to be nervous. I would appreciate it though if we could refrain from vulgar language as we are currently being recorded. Tammy, can you also scratch that from the record." The recorder went back and deleted the last line, smiling as she went.

"So, your names are Cassie and Terry Elm?"

Cassie answered this time. "Yes."

"Have you been informed of the risks due to this procedure?"

Cassie again, "Yes."

There were a few more general questions before the reviewer got to the point. Terry was fidgeting in his chair the whole time. "I believe, as a review committee, we are still unsure of the reasoning behind a IIa trial. May we ask what your reasoning is for committing to this trial? I assume you are committed since you traveled down here. We also have to say, that having the patients for a clinical trial attend a meeting is very unorthodox."

The reviewer gave Tripp an evil stare at this point.

"We have been told that. We apologize sir, but we really wanted to be here. It is our bodies after all. And yes we are committed. After seeing all of that good that Dr. Galloway and Stein have done for the sickle cell community, we couldn't help but wonder if he could help us too," Cassie said.

Aiden thought it was a good answer. Tripp and Morti were nodding. The woman at the end of the table, the one with the embryo question, was not. She leaned in and spoke, "That still doesn't really help us Mrs. Elm. I still don't know why you are committed. You are a carrier of CF, but are not suffering from it."

Terry cleared his voice and spoke up.

"Uhh ... it was our dream to have children. To teach them how to tie their shoes or ... watch them go to prom. We tried to have a baby but some of the tests that the OB-GYN ran were odd. Eventually, after some digging, we found out that we were both CF carriers. The doc laid out our options. The less risky options were out of our league, financially. If we kept trying to have kids naturally, we could lose one very young. The 1:4 odds or whatever they are weren't worth the risk of having a tiny casket at a funeral."

Terry kept going as the tears slowly ran down his face.

"The tiny casket is important because that was what my folks went through. I lost my brother, Caleb, when he was young. Freak accident. Nothing anyone could have done differently, just shit luck. I watched my mom stare at that tiny damn casket. Both my parents never really recovered. They were walking dead people, maimed on the inside. They were shells of their former selves. You can't imagine holidays after that. We just sat around really, stuck in our own brains."

The team didn't know the story about Caleb; it was heartbreaking. Tara and Michelle started to tear up while Tripp and Morti slumped in their chairs, morbidly staring.

Terry continued, "I didn't want that for myself, for Cassie. I loved her too much for that, to watch her die on the inside. But when I heard of Dr. Stein and Dr. Galloway from their first trial ... I ... I knew I had to try. They were our last hope. They still are."

Terry sat back in his chair and swiped at the tears on his face. He never let go of Cassie's hand. He couldn't, he was shaking. "Does that answer your question ma'am?"

The woman didn't respond to Terry. She merely sat back in her chair, apparently satisfied. The reviewer thanked the Elms and moved on to the technical side of the clinical trial. Tony took over and was questioned for another forty-five minutes. Afterward, the review committee excused themselves.

As soon as they left, Morti turned to Terry, "I'm sorry about your brother Terry, that's terrible."

"Thank you, it happened a long time ago."

Everyone said how great they did. How they really helped secure the future of the trial. Terry wasn't listening. He just wanted this meeting to be over. He just wanted a chance at having a baby.

8 JANUARY 2029

THE FOOD AND DRUG ADMINISTRATION

SILVER SPRING, MARYLAND

Fifty minutes had rolled by since the review committee had excused themselves. Aiden was starting to get a little nervous. It usually did not take this long to receive a recommendation. As time marched on, Tony tried to make conversation. No one was in the mood.

Another five minutes passed before the committee came back into the room. The head reviewer let everyone take a seat before he began for the final time. "After reviewing your meeting packet, we recommend that you continue your phase II trial with limited observations. Our liaison will send you the meeting notes and the observations."

He paused. "As for the phase IIa trial, we agree that a CF proof of concept would be beneficial, as animal models are limited. We would recommend with several observations that you proceed. You will also be receiving those notes. Congratulations."

Aiden had to admit, the reviewer had him going for a moment. Terry leaped from his chair and kissed Cassie. Hands were shaken and hugs were given. They could barely contain themselves as they left the building, Tony basically sprinting to the car.

He popped the trunk and whipped out a 24-pack of beer. "I think this is a perfect time to celebrate!"

Tara and Michelle laughed. Aiden shook his head and put his hand out. Cassie declined the beer.

"Hey, you have to drink this! It could be your last one!" Tony said gleefully.

She laughed and accepted. Cassie really hoped that Tony was right.

XXI.

LEE GOLDBERG BEGAN HIS BROADCAST cheerily, as he would any other day.

"Good Morning, welcome to *The Today Show*, it is a blustery January 17th and I'm Lee Goldberg. I'd like to start off this morning with some very special news. Savannah, do you remember Dr. Galloway? He was the man that helped to cure sickle cell disease."

"Yes, Lee I do. He was on the show wasn't he?" Savannah said.

"Absolutely, well he is at it again but this time he is looking to take down cystic fibrosis, can you believe it?"

"Wow, that's absolutely incredible."

"Savannah, I couldn't believe it either, so this coming Friday, stay tuned for the exclusive interview with Dr. Perfect himself."

Jodi couldn't believe it. After all of her work, all of her ambition, this man was still trying his best to undo God's will. She stood in the living room, hands akimbo, glaring at Lee babble on. *I can't let this stand. I have to do something. Monica has been asking me to come back.*

This is the perfect time. I'm the only one who can get a rally together that quick.

Cal sauntered down the stairs and looked at Jodi.

"Oh no, oh no, whatever it is, forget about it. The last time you were seriously watching Lee fuckin' Goldberg, you got into this whole vaccine mess." Cal had put his foot down after Jodi got hurt at the rally. He went along for a while, but after seeing his wife in the hospital, he went berserk.

"Honey, I can't forget about it. That doctor is at it again, trying to fix people with cystic fibrosis. You know how those people got cystic fibrosis? Do you? It was the TB vaccine. I read it online, I swear it. And now this guy is trying to fiddle with their DNA to make them better. It isn't right. God is shaking his fist right now, calling on his angels to act."

"You are not God's angel. You are my wife and the mother to our beautiful children. What are you going to do anyways? Lead your friends up there on some type of rally and get yourself hurt again? No, absolutely not."

Both were yelling at this point. Thank God the kids were both at school. Cal had taken off to fix the roof.

"I am doing this for our children. I am doing this for Jimmy!"

"You can't fix Jimmy! We've tried Jodi; you've got to let this whole Monica thing, this whole vaccine thing, go!"

"I can't! I just can't. Don't you see, this is what I am meant to do. God wants me to do this work. I'm the only one who can stop this man, this heathen."

Cal was worried. He had watched his wife over the months. She was getting more and more crazy about this whole vaccine thing. He was afraid there was nothing he could do.

"How are you going to stop him, Jodi? Kill him?"

She paused. No of course not. She couldn't do that.

"No Cal, I'm not going to … to kill this man," she said sarcastically.

"I am going up to Monica's right now, though, to draw up a plan. I'm packing my things right now whether you like it or not."

Cal was furious. "Why does it have to be this fuckin' way Jodi? Why is it your job? No one else seems mad about it except you!"

"Damnit Cal, I'm doing this for Jimmy! Can't you see that this is all for Jimmy! This doctor Galloway is trying to undo God's will, and I can't let that happen. Not for God and not for Jimmy."

Jodi trudged up the stairs to pack her bag. Cal followed her up.

"This is ridiculous Jodi. Please, please stay home."

She ignored him as she threw clothes in a bag. Her mind was racing. She needed to get in touch with all of her local protestors, contact the groups that were like-minded in New York and call Monica on the way over to her home. When she was finished, she turned to leave and saw Calvin in the doorway.

She walked up to him.

"Move Calvin."

"No."

"Move Calvin, if you love me you will move."

"Jodi, if I love you I won't let you do this."

"Move."

With a huff of resignation and a dejected nod, he stepped aside. He had lost to Monica. As Jodi was walking down the stairs, Cal called out. "Wait! Hold on, you're forgetting something."

He rushed to the closet and ran down the stairs, meeting her at the bottom.

"Take this, so at least I know you'll be safe up there at the rally."

He gave her a .38 revolver. It was a nice little gun with low recoil. You needed to cock back the hammer for it to fire, so there wouldn't be any mishaps.

Jodi looked up from the revolver and toward her husband. "Thank you baby. I really need to do this. I love you and I will see you when I get home."

She took the revolver, kissed her husband on the cheek and walked out the front door.

SILVER SPRING, MARYLAND

Dennis couldn't believe it. *Did Lee Goldberg really just say what he thought he said? How the fudge did they get a meeting without me knowing? How did this happen?*

Dennis whipped his cereal spoon across the room, splashing milk onto the carpet. Snowflake didn't even move, oblivious to her owner's stress. *How in the world was Dr. Galloway still pulling off his charades at the FDA?* It had to be Aiden, Dennis thought to himself. He knew that man was the only reason they got anything done.

Wrapping up his breakfast, he whipped off his slippers and raced to put on his shoes. He fumbled with the laces, frantic in his attempt to get to work. Dennis could not let this one go. The review members were going to hear about this, that was for sure. *Maybe Dr. Galloway and his gang should hear it too?* Now that was a thought.

What if he went up to New York and conducted an "investigation" at their office. Dennis was sure he would find something. It was brilliant actually. Dennis couldn't believe he didn't think of it before. *I'll get him after his interview. I can't wait to see his face and when I hand him those inspection papers.*

But first, he had to get to the FDA. He had to convince them to sign off on it all. After all, if they are going into phase II trials, an inspection was in order.

XXII.

SILVER SPRING, MARYLAND

DENNIS WAS LOSING THE ARGUMENT.

"Sir, they have an inspection coming up anyways and they need to be notified. I'll do the inspection and I'm going up to New York anyways; I'll drop off the notification."

His boss, Jerry, looked at him pathetically. The whole state of Maryland knew that was a lie.

"Dennis, you have to let this one go. We both know that you were not going to New York. You didn't even request the time off and no one would be able to look after Snowball."

"It's Snowflake. You know that if they pass my inspection, then the facility is perfect. Also, don't you think if the FDA is going to approve all of these highly risky trials, then we should at least put someone on the case that is dedicated?" Dennis was swinging for the fences here.

"I can't let you do the inspection as you already have shown you can't handle yourself in their presence." Jerry's patience was wearing thin. He couldn't believe they let Dennis keep his job.

"How about a quick day trip up there and I'll drop the paperwork off at the office? I'll even come into work that afternoon."

"Dennis, you and I both know that is basically impossible." Jerry was through with the conversation. "If you want to take the day off tomorrow and fan girl over the doctor's in New York, be my guest but you will not be bringing documentation from the FDA with you."

"Maybe I will take the day off tomorrow," Dennis said, defeated.

"Get out Dennis." He had been dismissed.

He left Jerry's office, feeling dejected.

Walking down the hallway and plopping down at his desk, he stared off into space.

Should I take the day and go to New York? Merely seeing me would be annoying to them.

Now that was a thought. He'll have to thank Jerry for the idea. He could go to New York and make sure that anything that was being done was still up to par, but from afar. Apply some artificial pressure.

Who says that the FDA can't duplicate their efforts in communications? They are going to send the email out anyways. Maybe I'll just bring a paper copy.

Dennis started clacking away at his keyboard.

"Now that's a good idea," Dennis said aloud.

He sent the communication to the printer.

I'm merely making sure the communication gets to them quickly.

"I'll have to request the day off," Dennis again said aloud.

"Denny, for the last time, no one cares. Stop talking out loud," the guy from the next cubicle said firmly.

"Sorry."

XXIII.

MORTI AND TRIPP WERE NERVOUS. *THE Today Show,* no matter how many times you've been on (Morti: 0, Tripp: 1), is nerve wracking. Makeup is flying everywhere, the lighting is bright and people are talking to you constantly, making sure you are prepared for the interview. Tripp was on his third cup of coffee, legs bouncing constantly. It actually made applying makeup difficult.

Lee Goldberg walked over, a bright smile on his face. "You guys ready to go?"

"Almost."

"Great, you guys will be fine. You know how this works."

"Lee, how long have you been on this show anyways? Does it take long to get comfortable in front of the cameras?" Morti asked. He always wondered how news anchors did it.

"I've been doing this too long Dr. Stein," Lee said with a laugh. He was called away to go over a final briefing before he could answer the question.

"Sorry Morti, next time," Tripp said. Morti was trying to get a photo out of Lee for his wife. She loved *The Today Show.*

"I just don't want to ask him outright, you know? I want to lead into it a little." Morti looked defeated.

"Oh, by the way, we have a meeting with Slavomir after this. I forgot to mention it."

Morti's face contorted for a brief moment, as if disgusted by the thought. "Just wonderful."

A lady in large headphones walked over to the both of them. "You guys are going to be on first, so let's get you in place. Follow me."

Morti and Tripp both complied. They had coordinated outfits today. Both were wearing navy suits with white dress shirts. The only difference was the tie color. Morti wore maroon while Tripp wore charcoal. They looked newsworthy, or so they thought.

As they got into position, Lee leaned over. "Did you see the protestors outside this morning? You all really know how to make a splash."

"Luckily, we were in the building before they arrived. We're going to try to sneak out the back after the interview," Morti said with some concern. He hadn't looked out the window.

"Sounds like a good idea. Ask Cathy what would be best. We won't address the protesters in the interview. Just the questions we went over."

"Okay great. Thanks," Tripp replied. He really did not feel like getting into why protesters are rallying. Their points of view are a little extreme in his book. He would never admit it publicly that their points are valid. He was after all, designing babies. He just thought they took it a step too far.

"Here we go," Lee said while turning toward camera 1. The man behind the camera was giving a silent countdown.

"Good Morning, today is January 19th and I'm Lee Goldberg. Today, as we mentioned previously during the week, we have two very special guests. Dr. Galloway and Dr. Stein from Galloway and Stein Reproductive Associates are here today to walk us through their new breakthrough on cystic fibrosis. If you remember folks, Dr. Galloway, or as we know him Dr. Perfect, was on several years ago to discuss how they had cured sickle cell anemia. With that, good morning Dr. Perfect and Dr. Love."

Morti felt the heat of embarrassment creep up his neck. His wife thought that nickname was hysterical. He did not like it so much. "Please, Dr. Stein is fine. I would much rather have been Dr. Perfect."

"I don't know, I think he got the better nickname," Tripp said.

"So, you both are now conducting a study to cure cystic fibrosis, is that correct? What can you two not cure?" Lee chuckled at his own humor.

"That is correct. We are currently in a proof of concept study that will show we can cure cystic fibrosis, just like we do for sickle cell anemia," Morti replied.

Tripp jumped in. "To answer your second question, we don't quite know yet what we can't cure. We're hoping to cure everything we can get our hands on to be honest. Once we cure cystic fibrosis, we plan on trying to create a platform that allows us to personalize our work."

"Now are you curing everyone with cystic fibrosis? And do you think you can cure everything? Personalizing the work sounds like a daunting task."

Morti fielded the question. "Unfortunately, cystic fibrosis can be caused by a variety of mutations and we are only focusing on the main one at this time. So, no, it won't cure all CF patients. And, yes, personalization is a daunting task but if we can make our work a little more accessible, we believe we can cure a lot more people."

"And what is cystic fibrosis or CF exactly?" Lee asked.

Morti said, "It's a genetic disease where both your mother and father have to give you the mutation. When you have it, the sodium channels in your lungs malfunction, causing mucus buildup. It makes breathing extremely difficult. It also produces some other symptoms, which all together, shorten the lifespan of the patient significantly."

"So how do you cure it? Can you run us through the process and are people already getting the treatment?" Lee was hitting all the questions, as expected.

Tripp responded next. "People are already scheduled for treatment to prove the concept. We are not opening this up to all patients yet, that would be in our next trial. We have selected a few people who are great candidates to prove our work. Once we confirm with the FDA that our cystic fibrosis process is as robust as our sickle cell process, we will be able to open it up fully. The FDA has been working with us throughout the trials and it has been great. The people at the FDA are brilliant."

Mission accomplished. He wanted to plug the FDA somewhere. He really wanted to keep them happy.

Morti fired off another answer, "Yes, they've been awesome. But to go back, we take an individual's bone marrow, and either extract or create stem cells from the marrow, edit the DNA, place the new cells into the patient via transfusion and voila, they are cured."

"Wow, that sounds too easy."

"Our team makes it look easy, let's put it that way. We couldn't do it without our top-notch staff." *Second mission: check*, Tripp thought to himself.

"Now our final question of the morning actually came from a participant on Facebook and we thought it was a very good question. Jessica from Seattle asked, 'What's next?'"

Tripp and Morti looked at each other and acted perplexed. They were already working on infertility for Senator Chester. It made sense to move forward with that through the FDA to cover their tracks a little. They couldn't say that on camera though.

"We don't actually know. You see, someone approached us about working on cystic fibrosis. We look for diseases that are inherited, and have specific mutations, so please, if anyone has any suggestions, we would love to hear them," Tripp said smoothly.

"We are in fact, primarily, infertility specialists, so our main objective has always been to help create families. We would love everyone to go to our website, though, and fill out a questionnaire. It could be a viewer that we cure next!" Morti said slyly. It was a great plug for the company.

"Curing disease in your spare time while creating families during work, truly great stuff. Thank you so much, both of you for coming on today, we will have to have you back to keep us updated." Lee wrapped up the interview.

"No, thank you," they both said together.

"We will keep you updated on Dr. Love and Dr. Perfect, and with that I will turn it over to weather."

Once the camera panned away, Lee leaned over, "Great job guys, that was perfect. Now Cathy, the woman in the green dress can help you out on staying away from the protesters."

"Perfect Lee, thanks again for having us on," Tripp said while beginning to stand.

Morti, seeing his only opportunity fade away, had to ask, "Lee, would you mind taking a photo with me? My wife is a big fan."

Lee laughed a little, "Sure Dr. Stein, next time you are on the show, bring her with you."

Tripp grabbed Morti's phone and snapped a couple of photos. He also made them act for a live photo. They both waved and said, "We love you Cheryl." It was perfect.

Lee had about thirty seconds before he was back on, so they shook hands and parted ways. Morti and Tripp made a beeline to Cathy.

"Right this way guys, we'll get you out of here, no problem."

Tripp and Morti trailed Cathy by a few steps as they hopped into the elevator and made their way through a cubicle farm. They walked toward a back corner where Cathy simply pointed. "Go all the way down and you will hit the metal exit door, that'll put you in the garage. From there you can walk out onto the street."

"Thanks Cathy," Tripp said while opening the first fire exit door.

Complying with the marching orders, Tripp and Morti walked down the stairs until they hit the garage entrance. From there they located the elevator that took them to the ground floor. Finally, they broke through to sunlight, like newborns, they squinted coming out.

"Where is our meeting at?" Morti asked. He hoped it wasn't far.

"Down by us. Hopefully we can catch a cab."

"Perfect. Now the hard part." Morti stepped up to wave down one of the million cabs zooming by.

———◆———

Dennis could not believe his luck. Just strutting up the street, with the inspection papers in his hand, Dr. Galloway and Stein basically fell into his lap. He could see them, trying to hail a cab up about a block. *I better not let them get away*, Dennis thought to himself. He picked up his pace, trying to ensure his minor victory. He NEEDED to see the look on Dr. Galloway's face.

Jodi knew they would not come out the front door. Not with her group here.

She was proud of her gathering. They were about fifty strong, which was significant with the amount of time they had. Thirty people from the Manhattan area had combined with the twenty people from Ludlow to create this perfect coalition. Jodi was amazed at her own work.

Just like the previous rallies, she split the group into two as soon as the interview was done. One group stayed toward the front while she led a group around the corner.

As she was rounding the corner, a metal door opened. To her surprise, Dr. Perfect and Love both walked out of the door, seemingly unaware of the mob coming toward them. The rage inside her was uncontrollable. Everything these men had done was too much to bear. They were taking away the chance of Jimmy having a normal life. They were mutilating God's work. Her pace quickened as if being lifted by angels, sent from the Lord above. He would protect her. She was sure of it. Jodi, feeling God's love course through her veins like hot fire, unzipped her fanny pack and reached for her cell phone. She wanted to record everything. Instead, her hand came to rest on her husband's revolver. Looking down on the piece of metal; a simple, efficient machine, it almost sparkled in the light. Jodi knew that God just winked at her.

On their way to see the doctors, Alex spotted the protesters lined up along the sidewalk. "Sir, do you see them?"

"Yes, turn around and pick them up," Slavomir commanded. He could not have his investments go to shit.

Alex promptly made an illegal U-turn while Slavomir texted Tripp.

"We see you. Don't move. Picking you up now."

Tripp's phone buzzed.

"Stop with the cab Morti, Slavomir is around the corner," he said while giving him their location.

In what seemed like moments, the Maybach slowed in front of them.

Seemingly from out of thin air, a woman approached while yelling nonsense. It was one of the protesters brandishing a sign that read, "God says NO to DNA edits".

"Oh shit," Morti let out. This wasn't going to be good.

At that same moment, Dennis started yelling from the opposite direction. "Dr. Galloway, Dr. Galloway, stop right there!"

Hearing his name Tripp turned around. With his back turned, the woman pulled out a revolver. Morti saw the gun. He tried to shove Tripp to the ground. But it was too late. The revolver exploded in the woman's hand, sending a tiny, hot piece of metal careening into Tripp's back, just above his right kidney. Morti was stunned. He stood frozen in place, watching his friend sink to the pavement. He couldn't process what had just happened.

"Shit, shit, shit, shit," Arkady said while throwing himself out of the car. It was almost instinctual. In one fluid motion, Arkady unholstered his pistol and fired. With perfect precision, he placed two bullets into Jodi's chest and one in her head. The woman was dead before she hit the ground. Arkady stepped over the target and immediately started barking at the protesters.

"On the ground, on the ground right now! Do it now!" he roared. They were now a prime threat. He scooped the revolver from the dead woman's hands as she bled out on the sidewalk. A couple of cowards ran away. Arkady almost killed the runners, but remembered that cowardice was not a crime in the United States. It was a damn shame.

Slavomir was screaming in Russian. "Get Stein. I'll get Tripp."

Alex did what he was told. Gun drawn, he practically picked Morti up with one hand and threw him in the Maybach. Covering his boss, he surveyed the scene. Arkady had the protesters under control. Sirens were in the distance. A man on the opposite side had pissed himself.

While Morti was flying into a back seat, Slavomir got to Tripp and rolled him over. The hole was small but he was bleeding pretty good. Slavomir stuffed his handkerchief into the wound, making Tripp scream.

"Oh good, you're alive," Slavomir said sarcastically.

"Is Morti okay?" Tripp asked. His vision was going in and out from the pain.

"He's okay Tripp and so are you. That bitch barely scraped you. The ambulance is on its way now and we'll get you to the hospital."

By this point Tripp had bled through the handkerchief. She must have nicked an artery.

"Get me the QuikClot and get out of here," Slavomir barked at Alex.

Alex ran to the trunk and pulled out the medical bag. He ripped open a little pouch with his teeth and handed it to Slavomir. Turning back toward Tripp, Slavomir poured the white powder on the wound, helping to stop the bleeding. He continued to apply pressure while Alex sped off with Morti, peeling out down the street.

Morti, going way too fast for his liking, ran his hands over his body, checking for issues.

"Holy fuck Alex, holy fuck." Morti was sweating. "Is Tripp okay?" he asked Alex.

"He'll be fine. I am taking you home. Don't speak to anyone, understood?" Alex said.

"Yes, I'll be fine." He was still trying to catch his breath. He put his head back on the headrest.

"Do you need help?" asked Arkady, not taking his eyes off the protesters.

"No, watch for the police," Slavomir fired back. He was having a difficult time keeping the blood inside Tripp's body.

Slavomir was also concerned about how he was going to cover all this mess up. His guards and his family had diplomatic immunity, thanks to Putin, but this did not give him free reign to kill Americans. He did not fault Arkady for acting though. It was the right course of action. Unfortunately, he could not corroborate his story with Tripp, since he was passed out on the sidewalk.

As the police and ambulance arrived, Arkady put his firearm back in his holster. He quietly spoke to the protesters. "If you move before you are in handcuffs, I'll shoot you before you get off the curb."

No one moved.

As the police and EMTs worked furiously to secure the scene, Dennis tried to dry himself. He felt ridiculous, patting his pants with paper towels. He had lost control of his bladder, watching the men shoot that poor woman. Dennis couldn't believe it. They so casually ended that woman's life. Yes, she did shoot Dr. Galloway. They didn't have to kill her though. It looked like they could have injured her.

The police officer stared at Dennis while he continued to soak up the piss that currently clung to his pants. The tall sergeant was judging Dennis, that was for sure.

"So could you tell me what happened while you do that Mr. Myers?" the officer asked while trying to maintain some modicum of professionalism as a grown man wipes pee from his khakis.

Dennis was pretty confused about what exactly he saw but tried the best he could.

"Well, I was walking toward Dr. Galloway and Dr. Stein from this end when a black car pulled up next to them. At the same time a group of protesters was walking toward the doctors."

"Do you know the doctors?" the officer asked. He was writing notes down in his notebook but stopped when Dennis mentioned the doctors by name.

"Yes, I have worked with them before."

"How so?"

"I work for the FDA, the Food and Drug Administration, and I was on their review committee."

"So why are you here now Mr. Myers?"

"I was delivering FDA inspection papers to the doctors. They have a facility inspection coming up."

The officer stepped forward. "Why did you feel the need to deliver those papers in person instead of their office?"

"It kind of happened by chance really, I was on my way down there when they came out from the building over there."

"So what you're telling me is that you just so happened to be on the street where our victim was shot, and you just so happened to be delivering papers to them, right after their big interview, and you have worked with them before? Is that what you're telling me?" Something was not adding up for the officer. His quick Italian temper was brewing just underneath the surface.

Dennis could not believe this officer. He thought that Dennis had something to do with all of this! That was ridiculous, absolutely preposterous! "Yes, that's what I'm saying sir. So when I got close to the doctors, I called out Dr. Galloway's name. I needed to give him these papers." Dennis gestured to the documents.

"Can I see those?" the officer asked, reaching for them at the same time. "You can keep talking."

Dennis was getting flustered. This officer was making him uncomfortable. "So when I called out to Dr. Galloway, the lady shot him in the back. As soon as she did that, three men jumped out of the black car. One man shot the lady and told all of the protesters to get on the ground. He was screaming. The other two guys were yelling in some other language, I don't know what it was. The one guy grabbed Dr. Stein and threw him in the car while the other guy tried to save Dr. Galloway. Or that's what it looked like."

The officer looked up from the FDA paperwork. "At what point did you piss yourself?"

"How is that relevant officer?"

"Everything is relevant when two people are shot Mr. Myers. Now, I'm going to need you to come with me. Your story isn't adding up." The officer started to turn Dennis around.

"What do you mean officer? Am I under arrest? I didn't do anything wrong!" Dennis started yelling, but the tall Brooklynite did not even care. He simply flipped the cuffs on the weak FDA guy.

"You're not under arrest; we are just taking you into custody for questioning. Now relax, don't make this hard on yourself. There is no way that you just happened to 'show up' at the attempted murder of your associate here. Aright?" The officer led Dennis to a cop car.

"You can't do this! I didn't do anything freaking wrong!" Dennis yelled. It was all he could do when the cop tossed him in the back of the car.

"I know Mr. Myers, they never do," The officer said as he closed the door and spoke to another patrolman. "Can you take this guy down for me? His story is off. Have him sit for a while and I'll be down there in a little bit."

XXIV.

BEEP ... BEEP ... BEEP.

My head is killing me. What the hell is that beeping? Did I get a sun-burn? I'm pretty itchy. Trying to understand what was going on, Tripp opened eyes only to be temporarily blinded by the fluorescent lights in the hospital recovery room. His heart rate spiked once the memories came flooding back. An intense pain in his back and Slavomir rolling him over. People screaming. The tunnel vision, which Tripp could only assume was him blacking out.

Alex, who had been sitting next to him the whole time, put a hand on his shoulder. "Tripp, you're safe. You're safe. Relax."

Tripp looked at him, surprised to see the giant Russian. "Alex, what the fuck happened?"

"You were shot. Morti is okay. The ambulance brought you here. You went to surgery. That's all I know," Alex said frankly.

That's when Tripp noticed the tightness in his back. His abdomen was wrapped up with a compression bandage, making it a little uncomfortable to breath. He must have needed serious surgery.

"Who shot me?" Tripp asked. He didn't even see the person.

"One of the protesters. Don't worry, Arkady got her for you," Alex said with a smile and a pat on the shoulder. He sank back in his chair, reading *Time* magazine.

Do I thank Arkady? Tripp thought to himself. The Russians saved his life. *I guess a thank you was in order for killing the woman.*

Looking around the room, he saw he had received flowers. Morti and his wife sent a bouquet. The team had sent one. So did *The Today Show*. They sent a huge bouquet actually. It must not be good for business if interviewees get shot after their show.

"Does Arkady like to drink Alex?"

"Yes."

"What does he drink?"

"Vodka."

"Of course he does. Remind me to get him a bottle."

At that moment, a pretty doctor walked into the room. "Ah, Dr. Galloway, I am glad you are up. My name is Dr. Tori Yamasuko, I was your surgeon yesterday."

The doctor had warm brown eyes and dark hair, tied up in a messy bun. Wearing green scrubs and bright pink Nikes, she was a sight to see.

"I guess a thanks is in order. My friend here wasn't so sure on the details, can you fill me in?" Tripp asked. He was curious why he had such a strong morphine drip. He had realized the headache and itchy feeling was from the drugs. He hated morphine. He'd rather have tequila.

"You came in with a GSW to your right posterior thoracic area, right above your kidney. The bullet nicked your renal artery. I had to go in and repair the tear, dig the bullet frags out from your ribs and intestine. You were under for quite a while. Not an easy fix. Luckily, someone had thrown QuikClot on your entry, which helped stop the bleeding a little."

Tripp looked at Alex. He simply said, "Slavomir" and put his head back in the magazine.

"Remind me to get him a bottle too," Tripp said back. He then turned his attention to Dr. Yamasuko.

"I don't know how to thank you Dr. Yamasuko, maybe coffee or something?" Tripp was shooting for the fences here.

Dr. Yamasuko laughed. "Don't thank me yet, Dr. Galloway. When this morphine runs out, you are going to be in a load of pain. I'll be back in a couple of hours to check on you. One of the nurses will be in to change the bandage. Other than that, sit tight."

It was worth a shot. Tripp thought to himself. His injury brought him close to death. The least he could do was try to make his mother happy in his dying breaths by trying to snag a date with the very attractive surgeon.

As the day moved forward, nurses and guests filed in and out. He wanted for nothing. But as the night closed in and Alex rotated with Arkady, Tripp retreated inward. Being politely rejected by the doctor hit him harder than he thought it would. Coming close to death and having no one but a couple of large Russians for company was becoming miserable. Tripp didn't think about his future or his legacy unless it was work related. This incident shook him. He had no one. No little boy to play catch with, no tea partying with his daughters. Not even someone to keep warm with in the dead of winter. Being alone in this hospital room made Tripp realize he was alone. Destined to live out his days, practically selling babies to couples. Tripp didn't know what to say. He didn't have an answer for himself. *I guess dating would be a start.* Tripp hadn't been on a date in years.

Shaking him from his morbid reverie, the nightly news was showing his crime scene. The title was *Terror at the Today Show*. Tripp had to admit, it was clever.

Flashing up on the screen was a picture of a middle-aged woman. Apparently, that was Tripp's would be murderer. Jodi-Ann Kapp was being labeled as an extremist. Tripp was reading the subtitles as Arkady was scrolling through his phone. Arkady looked up briefly and resumed his scrolling.

Jodi-Ann Kapp was shot dead by an unknown hero after she opened fire on Dr. Allen Galloway, otherwise known as Dr. Perfect. Dr. Galloway was giving an interview on The Today Show when he was shot leaving the building. Dr. Galloway was rushed into emergency surgery where it is said that he is in stable condition. The police are withholding the identity of the hero, citing an ongoing investigation. The police also stated that Jodi-Ann Kapp was a known anti-abortion activist from Mississippi who held extreme views surrounding gene editing and vaccines. Jodi-Ann, approximately six months ago, was involved in an altercation outside an Atlanta abortion clinic, where she was treated for minor injuries. As the story evolves, we will keep you up to date. This is Michelle Esteves, with NBC 4 New York.

20 JANUARY 2029

NEW YORK, NEW YORK

Dennis was wildly uncomfortable. He had been in a windowless room for twenty-two hours, thirty-six minutes and approximately forty-two seconds. He knew they could only hold him for twenty-four hours, hence the counting. He had given his statement approximately ten times. Dennis had called his lawyer, but the man was in Maryland. He was practically useless in Manhattan. So, Dennis had to wait.

It gave him a lot of time to think. He had been thinking for the past twenty-two hours, thirty-seven minutes and seventeen seconds at this point. Why did three random men jump out of a car and shoot the woman? How did they know Dr. Stein and Dr. Galloway? Did they even know them?

That was silly; of course, they knew them. How did all of them have guns? That was almost impossible in Manhattan. And what language were they speaking? That makes me think they weren't cops. They were also huge. Maybe military? The language, though. What was that freaking language? Maybe I can get the police report. Two of the three men stayed behind. They would have to give their names.

The whole situation was driving Dennis crazy. Looking at the clock again: twenty-two hours, forty minutes and fifty-three seconds. *What was that word that man was yelling? It sounded like draino. Dreamo? Trento? Dermo?*

As Dennis was throwing around different sounding words in his head, Captain Mikail Blatov entered the interrogation room for the first time. He was the last hope for the station to get any information out of this guy. He had turned out to be a real annoying pisser, no pun intended.

"Good Morning Mr. Myers, my name is Captain Blatov. I have a few questions for you if that's okay? If all goes well, we will have you out of here soon."

Dennis was not having it. "I am hoping it's in one hour and eighteen minutes Captain Blatov because that will be twenty-four hours. I don't know how many times I have to give my statement."

Captain Blatov was the ace in the hole interrogator. He had handled all types of loons before, even ones that leak body fluids. "I certainly hope so too Mr. Myers. Why don't you indulge me and run through the story one more time."

"You've heard it before. I was on my way to hand FDA papers to Dr. Galloway. He walked right out in front of me. One of the protesters shot him. Three men got out of a car. One man shot the lady. Another man grabbed Dr. Stein and took off with him in a car. The other man helped Dr. Galloway who was bleeding. The one guy who shot the lady yelled at all of the other protesters to get down on the ground. The other two were yelling in some other language."

Dennis stopped and looked at Captain Blatov in the name tag. M. Blatov. He started up again before Blatov could speak, "What's your first name Captain?"

"I generally ask the questions Mr. Myers," Blatov said confidently. He had several for Mr. Myers.

"I know, just indulge me for a second please, what's your first name?" Dennis was practically begging.

"Mike," Blatov said. He was still reading his notes and hadn't bothered looking up.

"Is that your full name? Michael Blatov?" Dennis was pushing.

"Mikail actually. I'm Russian. But enough about me, why didn't the FDA deliver the papers by mail?" Blatov was going to try and shake up the guy. He only had an hour to get an answer.

"I offered to deliver the paperwork since I had been on their review committee for their first trial. Do you speak Russian Captain?"

If he keeps talking I will keep answering, thought Blatov. "Do they normally let reviewers hand deliver paperwork? And yes I do."

Myers responded automatically, "No they don't but they wanted to get a jump on them because their trial is so high-profile. Unannounced inspections are common, you can check online or call my boss. Does the word 'dream-o' mean anything to you? In Russian?"

"That isn't a word in Russian Mr. Myers. I actually did call your boss; he said that you were kicked off this trial for, as he said it, 'biased behavior'. Can you explain that for me?" Blatov was narrowing his approach. After all, he only had fifty-four minutes left.

Dennis faltered. His lawyer said not to say anything that could get him in trouble. "The committee and I had a difference of opinion on the safety of the trial. What about derm-o?"

That caught Blatov off guard. Dennis had just cursed at him in Russian. *Der'mo* meant shit. "I would watch what you say Mr. Myers; *der'mo* means shit in Russian. And what was that difference of opinion?"

Dennis' eyes lit up. Shit. That made sense. When Dr. Galloway had been shot, the first man out of the car was saying, "shit, shit, shit, shit." They were Russian. *Russians with guns is an interesting combination,* thought Dennis.

"Mr. Myers, what was the difference of opinion?" It seemed Blatov lost the man for a minute. This guy had some screws loose.

"In the sickle cell anemia trial, they killed a person due to a blood sample error. I thought the process had too many areas that could have human error. They thought the risk was acceptable."

Dennis didn't care about Blatov anymore. He simply wanted to get out and search for Russians in New York. It was like searching for a needle in a pile of needles.

Blatov was running out of time. He decided to do some acting. He took a deep breath and slammed the table. He slammed in three more times: boom, boom, boom. Dennis looked shocked. Blatov roared, "No one cared about the difference of opinion, did they? Did they! It was only one person! They saved tons of lives after they steam-rolled you. You were wrong!"

"I was not wrong! They were wrong! What if it happens again, some good person will die," Dennis fired back.

"One good person to save thousands sounds okay to me." Blatov was making his move. Building up the piss boy.

"That's not right at all. The one person had a family, kids, a life," Dennis defended. He knew he was right. It was morally right.

"They gave their life trying to get a better one!"

"They would have gotten it too if it wasn't for Dr. Galloway." Blatov had Dennis boiling. He was reliving the argument all over again.

"It was Dr. Galloway's fault? How do you know? How are you so sure?"

"His signature is on everything! He had to check everything and he didn't. His crony Aiden probably signed everything," Dennis said. He really didn't like Aiden.

"So Dr. Galloway is a negligent fuck huh? He deserves what he got! Right! Right! Karma is a bitch," Blatov fired away. He had Myers now.

"Karma is evil, yea," Dennis said, leaning forward, eyes wider than ever.

"And you gave it to him. You delivered that karma with Jodi." It was the play. The final card.

Dennis sat back, puzzled for a moment. *Who was Jodi?* Dennis thought. He didn't know. "No I didn't Captain Blatov, and who is Jodi?"

Blatov was still yelling, he still had a shot. He tossed pictures of Jodi-Ann's body on the table. A corpse, riddled with three bullet holes. Lifeless eyes and bloodied, matted hair. "Your accomplice, Jodi-Ann Kapp. You don't remember her? You distract Dr. Galloway, she does the shooting. Nothing rings a bell about your friend that died? You pissed your pants Dennis! You pissed your pants because you watched your friend and any chance of stopping Dr. Galloway die! Die, Dennis. Simply, die."

Dennis started to cry. He had nothing to do with this. He was simply delivering paperwork. His anger got him into this mess. Sobbing, the haphazard mixture of hyperventilation and crying, filled the room. Blatov broke Dennis in that moment.

"I didn't do it. I was only delivering papers. I didn't do it," Dennis said between haggard breaths. It was pathetic to watch.

Blatov didn't think the pisser did it. He was too weak and too genuine. Might as well close this one out. There were forty-seven minutes left anyways. "Just tell me this Mr. Myers and you can go home. Why do you care what *dre'mo* means?"

Dennis kept sobbing. He tried to get it together but was having trouble. His cheeks were blotchy red and tears stained his button down shirt. After another minute or two, Dennis looked up. "The men that shot the woman kept saying it. They were Russian."

Blatov just sighed. This was a waste of his time. "Mr. Myers, I interviewed the guys, I could have told you they were Russian. You're free to go. You can pick up the report if you want in a couple of days."

Blatov left the door open and Dennis Myers simply staring in disbelief. Twenty-three hours, seventeen minutes, and ten seconds.

20 JANUARY 2029

NEW YORK, NEW YORK

Dennis stepped out of the precinct, squinting from the mid-morning sun. Tear-stained, and smelling of urine, he tried to get his bearings. New York City was very foreign to him. As he surveyed the situation, he quickly located a Starbucks on the corner. Making his way across the street, he ordered a warm coffee cake and a vanilla latte. Dennis normally stayed away from caffeine, but it had been a rough twenty-five hours, he deserved it.

While his coffee, if that's what you would call it, was being made, Dennis went to the bathroom. He flipped on the light and washed his hands and face. Coming up from the water he looked in the mirror. His hair was disheveled, eyes bloodshot and skin blotchy. He looked like a recovering alcoholic.

Dennis couldn't stand what he looked like. The doctors had done this to him. Dr. Galloway and Dr. Stein had put him through hell without even speaking to him. Looking in that mirror, it was evident that they had outplayed him every step of the way. He was always two steps behind. Watching his reflection, his breathing, his blinking, Dennis focused on the details, trying to understand how he could win. This is what it had come down to, winning and losing.

Stepping out of the bathroom, Dennis grabbed his latte and coffee cake and found a seat in the corner by the window, a rarity in Manhattan. Dennis hadn't realized how hungry he was until the first bite of his cake. He was ravenous. He hadn't eaten all day. Wolfing down the coffee cake, he started on the latte. Trying not to burn his tongue, Dennis looked around the bustling store. Couples sat, deep in conversation while groups of tourists squawked and snapped selfies. Others, like Dennis, simply sat and stared in silence, ensconced in their own reveries.

Staring out the window, Dennis watched a couple walk into the Starbucks, bickering in some unfamiliar language. It made Dennis think of the Russians. How did the doctors know those guys? Dennis could not let it go. It bothered him. The men were all huge, they all had guns and they all seemed very concerned about Dr. Stein and Dr. Galloway. It just seemed out of place to Dennis.

The small man from the FDA swirled his coffee, pondering his past day. The caffeine buzz crept up his neck and rested in the base of his skull. It laid there, vibrating softly, as if all of his cells in his body were buzzing at once with joy. Dennis normally hated the sensation; he liked to keep control of everything, including his cells. Today, though, he probed the sensation with his thoughts, letting the feeling take control.

With his final sips, Dennis decided he would look into the Russians more, just to satisfy his own curiosity. The Captain said he could get the police report, if he wanted it. So that's what he would do. Dennis stood and tossed his cup into the garbage. His biggest problem now was getting to his car.

XXV.

17 FEBRUARY 2029

JACOB'S PICKLES

NEW YORK, NEW YORK

TRIPP WAS SLOW TO GO UP THE STAIRS. HE had already pulled his stitches once in the past two weeks and wasn't keen on doing it again. Tony, being at the head of the table, spotted the doctor slowly making his way over.

"There he is!" Tony was joyful, his mouth filled with bacon. The table clapped joyfully while Tara jumped up and gave Tripp a hug.

"Easy, easy, easy," Tripp said. She was squeezing quite hard. "Don't mind me, I have to sit slow. Continue with the meeting. Aiden, can you get me a coffee please?"

It was clear that nothing had changed. Aiden motioned for a cup from the waiter. Turning back around, Aiden jumped back in. "So Tripp, we were talking about Terry and Cassie. They came in for the initial consultation last week. We discussed how we want to handle the possibility their children may be carriers. They do not want that. So, we are going to do a selective screen. If the bloodwork comes back normal, we'd like to proceed in March or April."

A selective screen is pretty straight forward. Just make sure the children aren't carriers by picking sperm and eggs that are not carriers.

"That sounds good. How are they doing mentally?" Tripp asked. He genuinely liked the Elms.

Morti stepped in. "Their names haven't been leaked, so they are doing fine. We asked them to keep the people that know limited. We don't need them having unnecessary ... uh ... pressure."

The team nodded. The last thing they needed was the Elms having protesters outside their door.

"With that being said, I have some news," Aiden said aloud. He paused for a moment. This was a big deal for him. "I have decided to take another position and my last day is in two weeks from this Monday."

The table went silent. The color on Jim's face vanished. He looked like he was going to pass out. Tara, Michelle and Tony all had their mouths wide open.

Michelle spoke first. She actually spat out words and some mimosa. "Where are you going? What are you doing? What about the trial? Why?" She kept going. "You can't leave; we've got something real good going on here. I knew it. I knew it. My life was going too well. You had to pull the plug, didn't you?"

She was getting teary-eyed. Behind all of the bickering and alcohol was a team that really did care about each other.

"I know it's sudden. I have been talking with Morti and Tripp throughout my decision making process. I'll be working as a policy consultant for a shipping conglomerate that wants to branch out. The trial is fine. I will have everything wrapped up before I leave and I have every confidence in Jim. To answer the why, it isn't you guys at all. You guys are great, I am just not growing professionally anymore. I need something new. I've gotten too good at this. It's Jim's turn to make the FDA his bitch."

Aiden gave Jim a wink. Jim snorted. He was really in over his head now.

"I will be popping in to check on you guys from time to time. I'll even bring goodies." He was trying to cheer up the girls. They looked pretty upset.

"That's a fucking bummer," Tony huffed. "To Aiden, may he grow professionally, stop wearing skinny jeans and come visit us poor fucks."

The brawny Asian winked and raised his glass.

Tara chugged her drink and slammed the glass. "I hope you didn't have any plans Aiden because now we need to celebrate."

She whipped her pointer finger toward Tripp. "You were late, you pay the bill."

She whipped back toward Aiden, "Get up! We're going drinking. Tony, Michelle, get up, we're blacking out."

Morti chuckled. The team was great. They also seemed to buy Aiden's lie. He was sad to see Aiden go. The man was a machine and more importantly, a good friend. Aiden was always there when Cheryl was angry or he needed help buying gifts, when he was losing motivation or dealing with his baldness. Aiden had called him a better looking Taye Diggs. Watching the quartet walk out of the restaurant, he felt a pang of remorse. The actions they were taking were for money, plain and simple. Morti wanted to back out every day. He just wasn't strong enough. More importantly, he didn't want Cheryl to get hurt. Slavomir would mostly likely go after her, if he tried to back out now. He sold his soul to the devil.

With a sigh, he turned to Tripp. "Slavomir found us another client. Some Israeli Cabinet member that is a carrier for Tay-sachs."

"A cousin of yours?" Tripp said dryly.

"Yea freaking my cousin Abraham, you ass."

Tripp chuckled. Although they are still on very rocky terms, they did have good banter. "How was your Valentine's day?"

"It was good. We went to that great Italian restaurant … uhhhh … Lupa. I had this sweet potato stuffed pasta covered in some brown sugar glaze. It was incredible. How was yours? Anything?"

Morti and Tripp both knew the answer. Once again, Tripp was alone. Instead of a glass of Tequila, though, he just took a Percocet and went to bed. Thank you Dr. Yamasuko. "With the stitches, I didn't think I could perform optimally. Didn't want to pull anything."

"I bet you just didn't want to waste the Viagra old man," Morti fired back.

Tripp laughed. He was getting old. He looked at his friend and saw the wrinkles, the slow stand from a chair and the bad knees. He noticed them because he saw them in himself.

"You should try again with that Dr. Yamasuko; you're no longer a patient," Morti offered. He felt bad for Tripp. Tripp was a good guy, besides the mortal mistake of making friends with large Russians. He didn't want his friend to die alone.

"Maybe. I see her again next week."

They both paused, both knowing that he wouldn't try again.

After the tension hung in the air a moment too long, the doctors both started to stand. Morti would be going home to Cheryl. Tripp would be going home to another Percocet.

19 FEBRUARY 2029

NEW YORK, NEW YORK

Aiden sat on the tarmac at JFK, waiting for his Delta flight to Moscow to take off. They were a little delayed as snow flurries came tumbling down. Aiden had never sat in first class before. It was much better than coach.

"I guess working for a crime lord has some perks," Aiden said to himself. Champagne in hand, he contemplated his soon to be new life as an "Executive Assistant," aka, the project manager for a highly illegal baby making crime syndicate.

If I had to guess the craziest job I was going to have, this would never be it. I'm on a plane to goddamned Moscow in February to meet my new boss, who is some Russian special forces shipping mogul. That in of itself is too much to process.

Lost in his reverie, he was brought back to reality by his cell vibrating. Digging into his pocket, he pressed accept when a blocked number popped up on the screen.

"This is Aiden."

"I was wondering if you were going to pick up. Did you make the plane?" It was Arkady; business as usual.

"Ah Arkady, hi, how are you? Yes, I made my plane. I'm sitting on the tarmac waiting for them to take off."

"Good. Alex will be picking you up from SVO. He will come get you, do not wait outside," Arkady said matter-of-factly.

"That's nice of him, but I can meet him on the curb if he wants."

"It is operational security to wait inside the airport. Please wait inside."

"I didn't realize but I guess that makes sense. I'll see you soon."

"Da." The phone clicked off.

I'm going to have to get used to this. Arkady and Alex are not Tara and Michelle. The plane started to taxi to the runway.

"Would you like another glass of champagne?" the hostess asked politely.

"I might as well. Thanks."

The plane picked up speed, beginning their ten hour and fifteen minute journey.

Aiden was sore. Ten hours in a plane takes a toll on you, no matter the class of seat you have. He breezed through security, which he thought was odd. He wasn't going to question it. Apparently, his new boss has the ability to make all travel pleasant.

He did what he was told and waited inside, but he did not have to wait long. Alex found him quickly.

"Come with me. How was your flight?" Alex said while pivoting hard on his heel and beginning to walk back toward the vehicle.

"It was fine but, Alex, what happened to your face?" The right side of his face was a nasty shade of green.

"Arkady, that fuck, kneed me in the face. Don't worry, we don't do that to first timers."

"Oh, I don't think I'll be participating."

"Why not? It would be good for you to know some things. At least the basics of Sambo and Judo. We won't even go into Krav Maga."

"I think I'll let you handle that stuff."

They had got to the car and Aiden went to hop into the front seat.

"No, only people who know Sambo ride in the front seat," Alex said wryly. He shoved Aiden a little toward the back. Apparently, the hulking Russian has a sense of humor.

"Oh! The Russians tell jokes."

"We are only given two per day. Communism."

"Oh, don't waste them on little old me. Where are we going anyways?"

"Slavomir wants to give you the ropes before you get settled."

"Show you the ropes Alex, show you the ropes."

"Why do I need to be shown the ropes? I need to be given them in order to use them."

"I don't know Alex, English is hard."

"Okay, Russian it is."

As they sped through Moscow, gliding past the Kremlin, Aiden looked around in awe.

So this is my new home? I wonder how much time I will actually spend here. I mean, it's freezing. I should also probably learn a little Russian. I doubt I'll be seeing much nightlife anyways.

Approximately thirty minutes later, Alex and Aiden had arrived and gotten to Slavomir's Moscow home. It was beautiful and modern. Rising high above Moscow, you could see the Kremlin in the distance.

"Aiden, welcome to Moscow! How was your flight? Did Alex show you around?" Slavomir was dressed in slacks and a sweater.

"It was good. Alex has been trying to teach me Russian."

"That's good! Already settling in. Come and eat. I want to get you set up before we show you your apartment."

Slavomir gestured to the dining room table. Spread across the dining room appeared to be a heaping pile of information. "Sit and listen. I will answer questions at the end," Slavomir ordered.

Aiden did what he was told, taking off his jacket.

Slavomir also sat down. Alex and Arkady watched from the breakfast bar. They had never seen Slavomir brief anyone on his own life before. They haven't had a new person in the inner circle for years.

"So, you will act as my Executive Assistant while also handling our affairs with Tripp and Morti. Let's start with the easy stuff. This is your new cell phone. We will destroy your old one."

Aiden went to interrupt, but Slavomir stopped him with a wave of his hand.

"Wait. You need a new phone because any business associated with me is confidential. The Russian government has been watching your phone since you landed. Now you will handle my schedule. I will not receive any more phone calls. They will come to you and be redirected to my phone. Here is your gun and your knife."

Aiden was now very overwhelmed. *I'm a gay man from New York. What the fuck am I going to do with those things? This was not part of the deal.*

Slavomir read his mind of course as the horror came across Aiden's face.

"Arkady will teach you how to use it. That is for safety purposes. You will probably not use it. These are your Russian papers. If you ever get into trouble, show them these and your Canadian passport."

"I am not Canadian," Aiden said. He had to interrupt on that one.

Rummaging through the paperwork, Slavomir found what he was looking for.

"You are when you are in Russia. Here. You will also be handling my wife's schedule. It is light, but we need to make sure that either Alex or Arkady are with her. So, you also manage their schedules I guess. Finally, here are the keys to your apartment. It is below my apartment. It is bugged, full disclosure. Inside your apartment you will find all the information you need to get caught up on the laptop. There are also maps of Moscow. If you need anything, phone Alex or Arkady. We leave Wednesday and I expect you to be up to speed by then. I am finished talking, you may now ask your questions." Slavomir sat back in his chair.

"Do I really need to carry the gun? Do I really need the Canadian passport? Does my apartment really need to be bugged? Is it video or audio or both? Where are we going on Wednesday? How often will we be in Moscow? Do you trust me to handle everything with Tripp and Morti? How often do you need to be updated?"

The questions continued for another five minutes before he stopped talking.

Slavomir patiently listened and then said, "yes, both, Spain, yes. Now if you excuse me, I have another meeting to take."

Aiden got up and went to visit his new home. *Shit, I better get to work.*

XXVI.

SILVER SPRING, MARYLAND

DENNIS HADN'T LEFT HIS HOUSE IN TWO weeks. He had been on his computer when he wasn't sleeping or feeding Snowflake. His living room was filled with pizza boxes and Chinese takeout containers. He looked like a hoarder. His nose had gone blind to his own stench. Dennis had become obsessed with the Russians and Dr. Galloway. It just didn't make sense. There was no possible explanation for why these men would know each other.

Dennis planned on staying in his house until he figured it out or went crazy. He was leaning toward the crazy. After seeing Dr. Galloway get shot, he was put on extended leave. It was not every day that you see your colleague, even one you dislike, almost killed. The psychologist demanded he take at least six weeks to recuperate. Dennis had a meltdown. He screamed on the telephone for a week, trying to get back into the office. While sitting at home, arguing with his boss to come back to work, the police report came in the mail. That's when it hit Dennis. He could use the time to look into the Russians! Dennis hung up on his boss when the idea came to him.

It started off casually at first. He plugged the first name into Google, Arkady Gugilev, and got nothing. He didn't even have a Facebook page. The next man was another story. Slavomir Krukov was all over the Internet. He was a Putin-friendly, Russian billionaire.

Another week went past and Dennis looked into Mr. Krukov. Dennis read an interview or two. Looked at his education and official job titles. He found the guy's wife. It wasn't anything to write home about.

In the coming weeks, Dennis dug deeper, becoming obsessed with Slavomir. He read articles, studied his companies, looked at every photo imaginable. Over three months of research led to absolutely nothing. Dennis had collected a photo album of Slavomir's life and an encyclopedic knowledge of the man, culminating in no further leads.

Sitting on his couch, petting Snowflake, Dennis was defeated. He was staring at the ceiling and petting his cat. *Maybe I can go back to work next week? This is a complete waste of my time. I really should shower too.*

Snowflake, in that moment, decided she had enough of the petting. She jumped onto the coffee table, knocking over a pile of photos. Dennis didn't move, he really didn't care at that moment. He had lost to Dr. Galloway once again. With a moan, he decided to take a shower; afterward, he would call his boss.

It took Dennis over an hour to simply take a shower. He was disgusted at the state of his bathroom. He generally cleaned the entire apartment twice a week. He hadn't touched the bleach in two months. Stepping out of the stall, Dennis felt a little light-headed. The combination of steam and bleach made for an unpleasant atmosphere to scrub yourself. He grabbed his terry-cloth robe and wrapped himself up like a burrito.

When he opened the door and stepped into the living room, Dennis let out a gasp. He realized how filthy his apartment was.

"Snowflake, I am so sorry. This is horrible."

Dennis pushed off the phone call to his boss he was dreading and grabbed a garbage bag. Room by room, Dennis filled garbage bags with empty food boxes and dirty napkins. He dusted, vacuumed, mopped, scrubbed and scrutinized for hours.

By 4:00 p.m. in the afternoon, he was almost done. He took a break and grabbed the phone. It was time to finally throw in the towel and call his boss. As the phone rang, Dennis looked at the pile of photos that Snowflake knocked over. It was bothering him, spread out on the floor.

"Dennis, how are you feeling?"

"I'm good Jerry; how are you?"

"I'm great. How can I help you? I thought you had two more weeks of leave?"

"I took your advice and really took the time to get my head straight. I think I have done that though so I am ready ... " Dennis stopped. As he was talking to his boss, he started to pick up the photographs on the floor. That's when he saw it: a little boy with his parents. The boy had beautiful green eyes. Some would say stunning, just like his father.

"Dennis did I lose you? Dennis?"

"On second thought Jerry, I will talk to you in the office in two weeks." Dennis hung up on his boss again.

His genetics were a little shaky, but a baby boy with bright green eyes would be rare when one parent had brown eyes and the other had mixed dominance eye color. He didn't know the exact odds, but they weren't good. The boy also had blonde hair, another recessive trait.

"Two in a row," Dennis said out loud.

An idea started to bubble up from the depths of his mind. It started to take shape, like when water boils in a teapot. The bubble started off small and floated to the top erratically, almost at random. But as he stared at the picture, of the little boy, the large Russian and his wife, the bubble grew and became steady. It eventually broke the surface.

"There is no way this can be right." He was almost too afraid to say it out loud. He took the photo to the computer, his leg wildly tapping against the desk.

"Come on, come on."

Clicking through the web, Dennis found what he was looking for. 1 to 2 percent. That was the amount of green-eyed people in the world. 1 to 2 percent. Now with Slavomir's wife having brown eyes, the odds plummet. The odds of the child having blonde hair too was very low, with the Krukov's both having shades of brown.

Dennis sat back in his chair. "I don't believe it."

Dennis began to sweat. The idea was insane. Did Dr. Galloway really edit a baby? Dr. Stein would never. He was too much of a moral man. He threw the photo at this screen. It was impossible. Not to mention, highly illegal. So illegal, they'd both be in jail for the rest of their lives.

"It's impossible." Dennis got up and went back to throwing out all of his evidence.

XXVII.

30 MAY 2029

LONDON, UNITED KINGDOM

SLAVOMIR AND AIDEN WERE IN LONDON.
Slavomir was not amused. The client was late. The positive news was
that the business had been progressing nicely. Senator Ashley referred a
friend who had referred a friend, which led them to a cabinet member
of parliament.

That cabinet member was late.

"If they are not here in five minutes, we leave," Slavomir said
coldly. He was not one to be kept waiting. Partly for his ego and partly
for operational security.

Four minutes and twenty-two seconds later, the Secretary of State
for International Development sat down.

"Thank you for waiting, we got stuck in a bit of a mess back at
the office."

"Thank you for reaching out to us. My name is Aiden and this is
my associate. How can we help you?"

"I'd like to have a baby but I am a bit older. I also have some odd
chromosomal disorders."

"Can you define odd?"

"Kabuki something or whatever," the cabinet secretary said offhandedly.

"That is rare for sure but it is something we can help with," Aiden said.

The cabinet secretary's eyes lit up. She had been told it was very dangerous and now this American was saying that it was possible.

"How though?" She was curious.

"At this point I think we should set some ground rules before going any further," Aiden said cautiously. This was where Salvomir usually jumped in.

On schedule, "Miss, we operate at maximum discretion. Our general policy is that any disclosure of our offer and our interactions without prior consent from us will lead to complete revocation of our agreement and our products. Do I make myself clear?"

"Of your products? You mean you would take my baby away?" She looked horrified.

"We would kill you, your baby and your entire family. We would also kill everyone you told and probably some other people for good measure. What we are doing is highly illegal and that is why we are referral based and expensive. This is a community of trust. You break the community's trust and everything, including the other children in this world, are in danger. Is it now clear?"

The woman gulped. The idea was clearly unsettling to her.

"I guess that makes sense, to protect the children."

"We need your explicit agreement verbally, right now, before we continue." It was Aiden's turn to step back in since Slavomir handled the scary business.

"Yes, I agree."

"Perfect. Now you've already been briefed on price and other conditions for moving forward. We may call you one day and we expect you to be compliant but that call, if it ever happens, will only happen once. Now, have you been told about the various other options that are available for you to choose?"

"No."

"Well everything really but let's start with the basics, boy or girl?"

"My husband wants a boy."

"What do you want?"

"A boy is fine."

"Final answer, I don't want buyer's remorse here."

"Boy."

"Great, let's continue. This could take up to two hours, so I would clear your calendar."

Three hours later the cabinet secretary left the meeting location knowing exactly what her beautiful baby boy was going to look like. Not just what he will look like, but his abilities in sports and his intelligence. She knows his proclivity for long distance running and sprinting, his physique approximately and his chances of developing high blood pressure. She knows everything about her future son.

She was now on her way to her local bank and transferring a very large sum of money using a routing number she will receive by calling a burner phone. She will then be making an appointment with an Obstetrician in New York City that is in line with her normal holiday schedule. She will never see Slavomir or Aiden again. The only person she will see will be Tripp.

All her husband will know is that a miracle doctor in New York City was able to give them the perfect child. Everyone wins.

XXVIII.

DENNIS WAS IRONING, PREPARING FOR HIS return to work on Monday. He wanted to look perfect. He had been away for far too long and wanted to make sure no one at work thought less of him. All Dennis had was his professional record.

Dennis was thorough. He pressed the sleeves and the ends of the shirt with precision. His pants received similar treatment. The details mattered to Dennis. He had found through work that lives hung in the details. Minutes, milligrams, mortality rates all mattered. Finishing off his pants, he journeyed to his desk to get a jump start on his emails. They would be overwhelming, if he left them until Monday.

Sitting down at his desk, he went to type in his password. Behind the keyboard was the photo of the Krukov family. He had left it on the desk, the child staring at him constantly. He couldn't get the thought of Dr. Galloway editing a child out of his head. He imagined some grotesque scene, where Dr. Galloway holds down a screaming baby, power drill in hand, digging a tube into the poor child's shins. Of course, that wasn't the case. Not that he knew anyway.

Shaking off the macabre image, Dennis began to trawl through his mail. Every few emails, his eyes would flick toward the smiling boy. Delete, delete, delete, stare. Delete, delete, delete, stare. About half way through his backlog, Dennis grabbed the photo. He stared at the little boy. He had to do something. If Dr. Galloway had really done the unthinkable, he needed to be brought to justice.

Was it worth ruining a child's life? That was a big question. Dennis didn't care about the doctors. They were in the wrong. This little boy though, he was merely a victim. He couldn't control how he was born. Still staring at the photo, Dennis realized if he did nothing, Dr. Galloway would keep going. There was nothing stopping him.

How though? How do we stop Galloway and Stein? Dennis fingered the photograph, flipping it back and forth. *I can't go to the doctors; they would surely deny everything. Besides, I have no proof. Their team wouldn't talk; they were practically family. That was the key: family. They needed to talk.*

"I'll be back by Monday," Dennis said, patting Snowflake on the head. He shuffled to the bedroom to grab his duffle bag.

XXIX.

IF THERE WAS ONE THING THAT SLAVOMIR hated more than political parties, it was political conferences. At least the parties served alcohol. Sitting in the Waldorf-Astoria, Slavomir was slated to be the luncheon speaker for the Thirty-Fifth Annual Joint Shipping Conference hosted by the Norwegians and the Americans. Slavomir didn't give a fuck about the Norwegians. He actually didn't like them very much. They all thought they were fucking Vikings. He only came to this particular conference because one of the cities he ships out of, Murmansk, is perilously close to Norway. He also did quite a bit of business with America, so, here he was, listening to a bunch of assholes talk about 'shifting political landscapes'.

Slavomir casually nodded his head as shipping heads bickered over logistics and customs rules. His talk had been a hot button issue since they served sandwiches and soda. Getting around customs officials was a specialty of his. In Russia and other corrupt countries, you pay them off. In first-world countries, you had to be more subtle. It was about relationship building, and some light blackmail. So, Slavomir threw together a discussion that was complete bullshit but legal. Everyone was up in arms. Slavomir didn't care that next time they wouldn't ask him to speak.

The Finns sitting on his left had generally remained quiet. Finland and Russia were very close in certain parts of the country and Slavomir liked the man to his left. They had a nice working agreement between their two companies, trading black market firearms under the guise of radio equipment. You can always hide metal in metal.

"Will you be attending the dinner after?" the Finn asked Slavomir.

"What do you think?" Slavomir said with a smirk. The Finn chuckled.

"Is your wife with you?" Slavomir asked the man.

"Mistress."

"Good, my wife likes her better anyways. Come over for dinner tonight and bring her. 7:00 p.m."

The Finn patted Slavomir on the leg and got up. Slavomir, very bored with the meeting, walked with the Finn toward the main lobby. As soon as they left the conference room, their bodyguards appeared by their sides. The men nodded and focused on the task at hand, having dealt with each other before. They only had to be wary with each other, not on high alert. The life of a bodyguard is interesting because your actions are based on the mood of your principal. So, Arkady and Alex could be friendly with the two svelte Norsemen next to them for now. If Slavomir became irate with the Finn though, they would have to kill the men or be killed themselves. For the moment, it was polite caution.

Slavomir and the Finn shook hands at the door, reaffirming their dinner plans for tonight. With a nod, the bodyguards and the Finn headed toward the elevators.

"Alex, please tell Anna we are having Albin and Sophia over for dinner tonight. When she asks about Helga, just say 'Sophia is more fun.'"

Alex nodded again. He didn't like Helga much either. The trio left the Waldorf through the front. As they exited the double doors, a tiny man started to run up to them.

"Mr. Krukov, excuse me Mr. Krukov!" Dennis said aloud. He was about three feet from Slavomir when Arkady whipped his hand into his chest, stopping him in his tracks.

"Do I know you?" Slavomir asked condescendingly. He already knew the answer. It was no.

Alex recognized the tiny man though. Something went off in his head that didn't sit right. He just couldn't figure it out.

"No sir, you don't but I know you. My name is Dennis Myers and I know Dr. Galloway."

Slavomir shrugged. "I don't know a Dr. Galloway." Slavomir began to walk to his Maybach, which was pulling up as he spoke.

"Yes you do sir because I saw you save his life." Dennis needed Slavomir to talk with him. It was the only way to stop Dr. Galloway.

A flash of recognition ran across Alex's face. "He is the guy who pissed himself," Alex offered.

Slavomir laughed out loud. "Is that true? My friend here said you pissed yourself when Tripp was shot."

Dennis flushed with embarrassment. He would never live that down. "That was me but Mr. Krukov, I want to talk to you about Dr. Galloway."

"I am very busy. Excuse me."

Dennis took a chance. He needed this man. "I know your son is different. You know what I mean."

Slavomir stopped. His voice changed from dismissive to cold. "Get in the car."

Dennis complied. He hopped in the back with Slavomir while Arkady and Alex got in the front. Arkady pulled away from the curb and set off, driving North.

As Dennis went to put on his seat belt, Slavomir removed the ceramic blade from his forearm. In a well-practiced motion, Slavomir stabbed Dennis in between the ribs that protected the heart. Dennis gasped, barely recognizing the fact that he was just stabbed.

"Dennis, no friend calls Tripp, Dr. Galloway. This means you are probably his enemy and are looking to hurt him. Unfortunately for you, hurting him means you are hurting me and my son. That is simply unacceptable." Switching to Russian, Slavomir crisply states, "Get rid of the car."

As Dennis took his last breaths, Slavomir wiped his blade on the dying man's forehead. It didn't really work, there were still droplets on the blade. With a sigh, he wiped the blade on the man's shirt. It was so cliché. When he stabbed people, he tried to mix it up where he wiped the blood. Slavomir looked out the window, wondering what he would be eating for dinner as Dennis spewed blood onto the carpet.

2 JUNE 2029

NEW YORK, NEW YORK

Alex was driving down the New Jersey Turnpike. Having thrown the body into the trunk, he was in the right hand lane, going 65 miles per hour. He drove in silence. His hands gripping the steering wheel, he constantly surveilled his surroundings. He had never dumped a car in New Jersey before. He was also trying to determine where to dump the body. You see, disposing of evidence was a delicate business. You had to make sure they wouldn't be found. He preferred acid but that wasn't readily available. Luckily, New Jersey was a coastal area with plenty of shoreline. He would simply dump the body in the ocean. Part of his military training involved large amounts of scuba diving. He would conduct a shore dive, and then weight the body so that it would never be found again.

Unfortunately, he had to get rid of the car. That was a shame. It was a nice car. That was straight forward though, disposing of vehicles. Report it stolen and destroy the vehicle using a healthy amount of bleach (for the blood), the car battery and some slight rewiring.

10 JUNE 2029

NEW YORK, NEW YORK

Aiden settled into his new role quickly. It was interesting but exhausting. He didn't understand how Slavomir kept this pace up. They had been to a dozen countries in under a month.

He appeared to have settled into a groove with Slavomir and the guys though. The Russians would workout in the morning, or what they called working out. To Aiden it looked like murder. Then, one of the guys would work with Aiden on basic self-defense or pistol skills. He was terrible but they insisted. He will say though, he was getting into better shape. Finally, they started their day; meetings, conference calls, emails, calendar invites, etc. Alex or Arkady would pair off with either Mr. or Mrs. Krukov and Aiden always went with Slavomir. It worked. Not to mention, Aiden had basically doubled his net worth in under a quarter.

As Aiden waited in their New York penthouse for Slavomir, he worked on the dashboards for not only the shipping company but also the editing company. They were doing very well actually. The editing platform for Morti and Tripp was working on its third disease state, male infertility (thank you Senator Ashley) and on their fifteenth client. The shipping company practically ran itself and Aiden had nothing to do with that anyways; he was just curious.

Slavomir came back from a meeting with Alex in tow. They were speaking in Russian. Aiden's Russian was also terrible, just like his pistol skills.

Once they had finished, Slavomir switched to English.

"Aiden, I forgot to mention something. Your friend, Dennis, passed away."

Aiden looked up from his laptop. "He wasn't my friend; he was more of a pain in the ass."

"Oh good, well don't worry about it. I just thought you should know."

"Wait, when you say passed away, what do you mean? Do you know from what?"

"Yes, I stabbed him in the chest when he asked about my son."

Aiden paused to process. He tried to say something, but no words came out, just a weird gurgling sound.

"He approached me last week and said that he wanted to talk about Dr. Galloway."

Aiden finally got it together. "Okay, and then what happened?"

"I said I didn't know him, and then he said that he knew Leo was an edited baby. So, I told him to get in my car, and then I killed him."

"I wish you let me talk to him first before you killed him. I would have liked to know how he figured it out," Aiden said quickly.

"Alex and Arkady are working on cleaning up any evidence," Slavomir said. He didn't particularly like his actions being questioned.

"His car and his apartment in Maryland?"

"Da," Slavomir said dryly.

"Wait, can you slow down and back up. So, he approached you?"

"Yes, I was walking out of the Waldorf and he came up to me, claiming to know Dr. Galloway."

"Okay, and then what."

"I said I didn't know a Dr. Galloway. He said I watched you save his life, then we recognized him from when he pissed himself after the shooting."

Aiden nodded, urging him to continue.

"Then, I went to walk away and he told me he knew that my son was special and that he knew Tripp was involved. So, I asked him to get into the car, and then we got rid of him."

Aiden was still taken aback. "Do you know how he figured it out?"

"No, and we may never know. Alex and Arkady are going to do some searching to make sure we are fine. If not, they have been instructed to handle it."

"Wow, okay. Can they clue me in when they are done? I'd like to see if there are some learnings here."

"Da."

XXX.

TRIPP SAT NEXT TO CASSIE AND TERRY IN A crowded gymnasium. Up on the stage, little boys and girls sang and clapped, excited for their first big step in the world. Tripp looked at the stage in awe. Christian Francis Elm was about to receive his Kindergarten diploma. Terry was beaming, holding the video camera as high as he could get it. Cassie held her phone, recording every second.

Tripp sat and watched the spectacle. It was his very first Kindergarten graduation. Second actually, but he didn't count his own. It was amazing how time flew by. Just yesterday Tripp had delivered their healthy and happy baby boy.

The little boy now stood on stage, waving to his parents. Cassie began to tear up. She never thought this day would be possible. *The boy is tall for his age*, Tripp thought. He stood a head taller than the other children. *He must have good genes. I'll have to ask Morti when I get back about that.* Offering people a height option would be an added benefit.

Morti and Tripp had done fantastic in the past six years. The FDA had fully supported their expansion into other disease areas after

Christian was born. He was actually the deciding factor. Holding a baby in your hands when you begin Stage III discussions is a powerful image. They were doing so well that they had separated the gene editing portion of their firm into another completely separate company. The office couldn't hold all of the samples and patients anymore. Morti, Tripp and Tony split a Nobel Prize for their work. They gave all the money to Tony. Morti and Tripp surely didn't need it.

Tripp was now the CEO of GS Editing, and Galloway and Stein Reproductive Associates. The companies did fine but not nearly as well as the designer baby business. GS Design, as they called it at unofficial meetings, was their most profitable venture to date and still very illegal. Aiden, the *de facto* CEO, had created a network so vast and powerful that Morti finally stopped worrying about the legal ramifications. A quarter of the world's elite now had a GS Designs child. Their clientele included athletes, senators, rock stars and presidents.

The best part was, their secret was kept safe. Slavomir had implemented a strict secrecy policy. It was simple: talk and everyone dies. Tripp had to admit, it was brutal, but effective. In the time that they had been creating children, they had two security leaks. Slavomir took care of both of them. The first was Dennis Myers. Tripp felt bad about that one. He imagined Dennis thought of himself as a hero, trying to preserve the morality of science. The second was a Russian arms baron. The man tried to tell a reporter. Slavomir killed the man and his entire family. Since the event, he shows the photographic evidence to everyone who signs up for a child.

Sitting in the uncomfortable folding chair, Tripp stared at the children on stage. He wondered if any other children were created by him. He'd look into that too. The Elms would want to know. The graduation ended with a song. Christian ran over to his parents and gave them a big hug.

"Christian, say hi to Dr. Tripp!" Cassie said while hugging her little boy.

"Dr. Tripp! That's a funny name!" the little boy said instead.

Tripp laughed. "You're right Christian, it is a funny name. It's actually my nickname!"

"What's that?" The little boy didn't have a nickname.

"It's a name people call you instead of your real name. I got mine because I was the third person in my family. Tripp stands for triple," the doctor said, kneeling to get on the boy's level.

"Ohhhhhhhh," he said with wonder.

"Why don't you take a picture with Dr. Tripp, Christian," Terry said, readying his camera.

"Would you mind?" asked Cassie.

"Not at all, as long as you send me a copy."

He actually did mind but couldn't say no. He created this kid and the Elms were a tremendous help to him. With a half-hearted smile, Tripp posed.

"Now, we would love it if you joined us for dinner," Terry said. He squinted at the camera screen, checking the picture quality. Apparently, it was up to snuff.

"I can't. I really need to get back to the office. Thank you for inviting me though, this was awesome. Congrats big guy!" Tripp rubbed Christian's head and said his goodbyes.

The doctor made his way out of the gym and into the parking lot. Spotting his car, he autostarted the engine and checked his emails. He could hear his Audi S5 purring on a warm day. Approximately twenty feet away from the driver's seat, a wave of nausea rushed over him. Stopping dead in his tracks, Tripp put his hands on his knees. He started to drool. *Am I going to hurl right now?* This was scary. He hadn't thrown up in close to a decade. Another wave rolled over him. Putting his hand on a minivan, he threw up onto the asphalt, splashing his Cole Haan monk straps. Spitting into the pile, Tripp stood up. "Fuck," he said aloud.

Standing to his right was a little graduate, staring at him. He wiped his face and walked the rest of the way to his car. "Fuck."

XXXI.

MORTI AND TRIPP SAT IN MORTI'S HOME. Tripp didn't visit often enough. The house was gorgeous, a restored brownstone, exposed brick and hidden details mixed to form a warm atmosphere. Today was different; a chill ran down Tripp's spine. He had already read the tests. He was fucked.

Ever since the graduation, Tripp had been nauseous and light-headed. Eating was a struggle. He popped Tylenol like they were skittles. Extra strength, PM, with codeine: you name it, Tripp took it. Morti was getting concerned and ordered some tests for him. The results came back.

"Tripp I'm sorry; you need to go see someone. I know a guy uptown. He's an ass but the best." Morti looked up from the paperwork. Staring at his friend, he did not know how to comfort him. "Is there anyone I can call?"

There wasn't anyone he could call. Tripp was estranged from his family by this point. His work consumed him. The only people he had were the team and Morti. "No, no there's no one."

"I'll call the guy right now." Morti stood up and went to make the call.

Pancreatic cancer was not really something people survived. Correction: it was a fucking death sentence. Depending on how early they caught the progression, he might have a slight chance at survival. He had a better chance at winning the world series by himself though. Tripp sat, staring at the paper that was his unofficial death certificate. He could hear Morti in the other room, muffled tones hinting at the morose.

Tripp couldn't take it. He left, not bothering to close the door behind him. He set off to his home, which was on the opposite side of Manhattan. He decided to walk because, fuck, what did he have to lose. He walked through Times Square and Central Park. He gave the homeless guy a hundred bucks. He should have given his house to the homeless guy too.

It took Tripp two hours to walk home. He stopped on the way, buying a bottle of Ketel One and a bottle of Jose Cuervo Gold. He always liked dirty tequilas. He wanted to feel the burn. Walking up his front stairs, he left the door open. He grabbed a coke from the fridge and plopped onto the sofa. Mixing a Jose and coke, he chugged half of it.

He looked around his place. It was beautiful. The high ceilings, fireplace and floors were spectacular. Even the molding was simple, yet beautiful. The kitchen: spotless.

It all meant fucking nothing. Absolutely fucking nothing.

Tripp got up and grabbed the whole case of coke from the fridge. He wasn't moving until the Jose was gone. Pouring himself another one, he thought about his life. Morti, his only true friend, who kept calling, was basically ashamed by his actions. He didn't have anyone else except Morti. He didn't even have a cat. He didn't have any kids or a lover. Tripp didn't even have a regular hooker that he slept with. The need for companionship had plagued him every day, yet Tripp did nothing. He focused on his work. His sole love was the empire he built. When he was dead, though, people would forget. They would forget the great work that Dr. Allen Galloway had accomplished. They wouldn't even remember his name.

"Dr. Perfect," Tripp snorted, "More like Dr. Pathetic."

As the sun set, Tripp finished his sixth Tequila and Coke. Morti had left fourteen text messages and ten voicemails. Eventually, he stopped calling. The silence crushed Tripp. It slowly pressed on his chest until Tripp could barely breathe. He threw up his troubles, simply rolling over on the sofa and vomiting next to himself. He washed out his mouth with more tequila and a swig of coke.

On his seventh coke, his bender was interrupted by a loud knocking on his door. He didn't bother to get up. Whoever it was could take what they wanted.

Arkady, Alex and Slavomir walked into the house with guns drawn. If you left your door open in Russia, you were probably dead. When Alex spotted Tripp, he covered his nose. The room had started to smell.

"Jesus, Dr. Tripp, what the fuck is wrong with you," Arkady yelled.

Tripp looked up at them. "Oh boy, I'm glad you boys are here, sit, sit. Don't sit there, over there, though." Tripp was slurring. He stumbled into the kitchen and grabbed the Ketel One and three glasses. "I hate drinkin' alone."

The men didn't sit. They watched Tripp spill vodka on himself while he tried to make them a drink. "Here. Here! Fuckin' drink up motherfuckers. It's not the first time you fucks have probably drank with a dead man." Tripp slammed back his drink and made another one.

"Tripp, what are you doing?" Slavomir asked. He had never seen the doctor like this before.

"Drinkin', what does it look like?"

"Yes, but why?"

"I bet Morti already told you, asshole can't keep his mouth shut," Tripp said angrily. The look in his eyes was a mixture of pain and alcohol.

"You are correct, Dr. Stein was worried and gave us a call. I don't think you should be drinking with your pancreas in poor shape Tripp."

Tripp laughed. The Russian was giving the doctor health lessons. That was a first.

"So, I ask again Tripp, why are you doing this?" Slavomir had very little tolerance for drunk fools.

Slavomir stared at Tripp. He felt sorry for the man. No one should have to die this way. It was barbaric, having your insides betray you.

"I'm dead anyways," Tripp said. He knew he was dead. "I have nothing Slavomir. Nothing. No friends, no family, no baby, no nothing! This fuckin house, the job, it means jack shit!" Tripp flopped onto the couch, splashing coke onto the cushion. He started to cry.

"I don't want to die. I don't want to rot from the inside." His tears mixed with his drink, sloshing back and forth.

"What do we do?" asked Arkady. Normally, he shot people when they begged for their lives.

Slavomir didn't have an answer. He just kept watching Tripp sob and drink. The man who gave him his child was dead and gone. All that was left was this shell of a man.

"Just fuckin' kill me," Tripp whispered.

"Excuse me?"

"Just ... fucking ... kill me!" Tripp roared. He heaved himself at the couch and toward Slavomir. Slavomir slapped Tripp in the head, sending him to the floor.

"Tripp, I am telling you right now, I am not going to kill you."

Tripp picked himself off the floor and propped himself up against the kitchen island. He kept sobbing. Slavomir stooped to Tripp's level.

"You need to get your shit together Tripp; we need you."

"Why? So I can work for less than six months and die a painful death. No Slavomir, go fuck yourself." Tripp spat at Slavomir.

The burly Russian calmly wiped his face of the tequila-laden phlegm ball. He took his pistol out of the holster and ejected the magazine. He emptied it and placed one bullet back in. Slamming the magazine home, he pointed the handle toward Tripp. "You want it? You want to die? Do it."

Tripp stopped crying. He tilted to one side and corrected his balance. He couldn't sit straight. Did he really want to kill himself? Tripp sat there, silently looking at the matte piece of machinery.

Slavomir grabbed Tripps hand and slammed the handle into his palm. He wrenched Tripp's hand toward his forehead and pressed the barrel into his temple. "You want to fucking die you fucking pussy! You want to fucking die! Fucking do it. Get it over with! I'm sick of your pussy bullshit Tripp. Now what will it be huh? Here's the fucking door."

Slavomir slammed the barrel into Tripp's head over and over. Standing up, Slavomir kicked Tripp in the ribs. He grabbed a vodka-filled glass and tilted it back. Slamming the glass on the table he looked down on Tripp. "I'll leave the gun here if you change your mind. Otherwise, you have a meeting with a British Naval Admiral tomorrow at noon."

Arkady, Alex and Slavomir left Tripp on the floor.

2 JULY 2035

NEW YORK, NEW YORK

Tripp was a wreck. He had really spiraled out of control. Slavomir was very close to ending the man's misery himself. Slavomir thought the pep talk he had given Tripp a couple of days ago would help. It did not.

Slavomir, Morti, Tripp and Aiden met after hours in the conference room of their practice. Alex and Arkady spread themselves out amongst the office, casually observing but not intruding on the conversation.

"So, what are we going to do for Dr. Tripp here? Morti, what is the prognosis?" Slavomir asked the doctor.

Morti was also a wreck. He was losing his best friend. It was hard for him. He never thought this day would come.

"To be honest, the prognosis is not good. Pancreatic cancer is basically a death sentence, even with everything we know about DNA editing."

"Have we looked anyways, to be sure?" Aiden asked.

Tripp was already tipsy. "Yep, we looked. The tRNA is all fucked up."

"Morti, could you translate that for the Russians in the room," Slavomir said about himself.

"So, DNA makes RNA and RNA makes proteins. That is the real cycle of life. If you interrupt the cycle, you generally have problems. In Tripps case, the transfer RNAs, or the RNAs that link the protein building blocks together, are grabbing the wrong protein blocks, effectively causing chaos. This issue has also spread to other areas of his body. We may have been able to do something earlier, but we never caught it until Tripp started to feel unwell."

If he just went to the damn doctor for his physical, it would have come up on his blood work. Fucking idiot. Morti wasn't going to bring that up now; it was too late.

"So, there is nothing we can do?" Aiden was really grasping at straws.

"Nope. I'm a dead man." Tripp wasn't wrong.

"Morti, will you be able to handle the editing business yourself?"

"Slavomir, Tripp is in the room," Aiden said quietly.

"So what? He knows he is going to die. His legacy doesn't have to." Slavomir had a point.

"He's not wrong, I mean, I have no children, no wife, this is all I have."

"I need time to think about it," Morti said firmly. He knew this was coming ever since he read Tripp's blood work. He knew that he was going to have to make this decision.

"You have until we bury him." Slavomir stood up. "Do you want to be buried anyways?"

"Yes, my family has a plot back at home. I'll be laid to rest there."

"Then, it is settled. Morti, Aiden will be in touch. Tripp, you'll be sober for all your appointments, yes? Actually, that isn't a question. You will be sober. Happy Independence Day."

Slavomir got up and left the conference room.

"I'm sorry, Tripp. Morti, I'll call you." Aiden got up and left too.

Tripp and Morti looked at each other and sighed.

"Drink?" Tripp asked Morti.

"Sure Tripp, sure."

XXXII.

AIDEN WAS IN THE CAR WITH ARKADY. THEY were on the way to pick up Alex and Slavomir from another meeting with the Finns. They were not having dinner because Helga was in town and not Sophia.

"I'm going to give Morti a call, just FYI," Aiden said while dialing.

"Just make the call and save your words, you do not have to announce the call," Arkady said with a smile on his face. Arkady pretended to be bothered that Americans announce what they are going to do before they do it.

"Yep, sure, no problem Arkady."

They had developed a good working relationship. They were nice enough guys when not intimidating, blackmailing or killing people.

"Hello?" It was Morti and he sounded a little tired. Everyone was trying to be with Tripp as much as they could, despite his incredibly erratic behavior. The man was not dying with grace but who could blame him?

"Hi Morti, it's Aiden. I wanted to touch base privately since the last time I saw you was a little jarring to say the least."

"Tell me about it. I'm in over my head Aiden. It's getting bad."

"I know, I've been thinking about it, though. I think you sell the OB/GYN practice, legitimize GS Editing, the platform, and then you can outsource that to the team and keep the baby editing on the side as your piece."

"I was thinking of just downsizing the whole thing and retiring to Costa Rica." Morti had already been looking at properties. He was getting tired. He was also thinking of his wife.

"You know that can't happen. We need to expand the circle, bring Tony in or something," Aiden said.

Morti laughed. "You know damn well we cannot bring in Tony. He's a goon."

"I know but I'm worried about the continuity of the business." Aiden was putting that mildly.

"You mean you are worried I am going to die next," Morti said bluntly.

Aiden went silent. That is what he meant, but he didn't want to say it out loud. He tried a different approach.

"Look, if we can get a transition plan in place that Slavomir will buy, we can start to phase you out, so we can get you to Costa Rica. We just thought we had more time." Aiden was trying to find some middle ground.

"We don't. Tripp is already scaling back his work and not taking on any new legal clients." Morti was right again.

"I get that, so I'm trying to think of options here. Help me out Morti. I'm in fucking Finland right now trying to make this work. Do you trust anyone else? Any young, new doctors?" Aiden asked.

Morti thought for a minute.

"Look, Tara is telling me to hurry up. We can probably find someone from the OB/GYN program at Columbia. Maybe two people. Let me think about it."

"Okay, well, think quickly."

Aiden was mad. Morti was dragging his feet and not being helpful.

"I guess that didn't go so smooth?" Arkady said.

"It could have been smoother," Aiden huffed.

I'm going to have to put together this whole transition plan by myself.

10 AUGUST 2035

NEW YORK, NEW YORK

Tripp was pouring himself a vodka. He had just gotten off the phone with a hospice company. Planning your death was not a fun activity and today was dedicated to that morbid affair. Any minute now, Aiden, Slavomir, and Morti were going to roll in to discuss what to do after his death. He couldn't believe they still included him in these things.

"Out of fucking pity," he mumbled to himself while swigging his third vodka of the day.

I can't believe that DNA is what's going to kill me. Not the Russians. My own DNA betrayed me. Ridiculous. I edit DNA for a living and DNA is what kills me.

It was ironic that nature's own editing software is what would ultimately end up killing Dr. Tripp. When evolution or the editing of DNA goes awry, we get cancer.

The door opened and in came the five men.

Tripp started pouring vodkas.

"Can you put something in mine, besides vodka?" Morti asked.

Tripp said sure and dropped an ice cube in.

Morti rolled his eyes.

Aiden started. "Okay, I have a plan and it may work. I need everyone's okay, and then Arkady, Alex and I will handle the rest. Tripp, I'm sorry in advance for speaking about you like you are not here."

"No problem, I'm halfway out the door anyways," Tripp remarked.

"Okay, I've put together a three-year transition plan for both Morti and Tripp but mostly Morti for obvious reasons."

Slavomir let out a snort.

Aiden simply continued, "We will be selling the OB/GYN practice completely and starting a non-profit looking to cure all diseases with Morti and Tripp's editing platform. We will have a fully legal team. We bring on OB/GYN's from the Columbia program. Morti, that was a good idea."

"Thank you."

"You're welcome. While we set this up, Alex and Arkady will screen the Columbia docs to ensure we pick someone who is okay with being a little shady. In the meantime, we start to lean on our political connections to legalize pieces of our business. Including the pure cosmetic portions. This will give us some cover. This way we are able to get the ball rolling on legalizing the entire business."

"When do I get out?" Morti asked frankly.

"As soon as we can get the cosmetic portions legal, we will make the transition from working with you to the new doc. They will have cover with the cosmetic portions, and then we will work to get everything legalized."

"I don't like this whole idea of a new doctor. Too much risk," Slavomir chimed in.

"I know but we need to make the transition anyways. We can call it advanced product development for the commercial end of the business. There has to be a legal exemption we can get for the new doctor to work under. They won't even meet you, Slavomir. They'll just receive a paycheck." Aiden knew he was onto something. They hadn't particularly used any of their political connections.

"I like it; where do I sign?" Tripp said with very little enthusiasm while he inverted a Ketel bottle.

"Why don't you switch to Popov? It's cheaper and comes in a bigger bottle," Slavomir said while glaring at Tripp.

"I don't need the money."

"If everyone is in agreement, I would put the plan in motion today, starting with selling or closing the OB/GYN practice. I recognize that we need to take the pressure off of Morti since Tripp basically stopped going into the office."

"I mean, fucking look at me."

Tripp wasn't wrong, he looked like a skeleton and was chomping on Vicodin, CBD gummies and vodka regularly.

"So, let's take a vote then. All in favor?" Aiden asked. Everyone casually put their hands up. It was settled. There really wasn't any other way to handle this.

Feeling comfortable with the plan, Slavomir said, "Good. Aiden, please handle this. Morti and Tripp, we expect signatures by the end of next week. Tripp, don't die yet. I'll call our friends and get the political landscape to change."

Slavomir downed his vodka while Aiden left his on the table.

"Don't mind if I do," Tripp whispered to no one in particular while grabbing the full glass.

"You need to slow down on all the substances," Morti said, swirling his glass.

"Why? I called Hospice today. It'll be cheaper this way."

"Don't say that Tripp; there are people here who care about you."

"At this point Morti, I understand that but just don't care. I'm going to end up back in fucking Ohio, six feet under, next to my brother."

"Go out with a little fucking grace. You have saved more people than anyone in history."

Tripp started hacking. He couldn't stop. Morti got up and rubbed his back. It was pointless. Like fighting the wind.

XXXIII.

THE WALLS WERE A CREAM COLOR WITH A very okay looking navy floor. The Hospice facility had seen better days.

Aiden and Morti were sitting with Tripp as he continued to open his morphine line all the way.

"You need to stop doing that or the nursing staff is going to take you off the drip," Morti said matter-of-factly.

"They can fucking try. What are they going to do in reality? Kill me? Ha."

Aiden had been watching them bicker for hours now. They were like an old married couple.

"Enough please, Tripp, try to get some rest."

"I'll get plenty of rest soon enough, let me antagonize Morti for a little while longer." *That's all I have left,* Tripp thought.

Tripp closed his eyes for a brief instant. He had been restless for days, lying in the cold hospice facility, waiting to die. *I really fucked myself in the end, didn't I? I guess it's too late for regrets now. Nothing I can do about them. I should have at least tried to have a family.* He didn't know why the family portion was bothering him so much. He had a family, opening his eyes, there they were in his room, casually flipping through magazines.

"Hey Aiden, you ever think you'll have kids?" Tripp asked.

Without looking up from his magazine, "Not in fucking Moscow."

Morti snorted. "Why? What's up?"

"Nothing, nothing, I was just thinking about Aiden dressing his kids up in the hottest toddler designers," Tripp said dryly.

"Damn right I would."

"You have to stop beating yourself up about this kid stuff. You've helped thousands of people create families. It just wasn't in the cards for you. You think too much to have kids," Morti offered.

"What does that mean?"

"The majority of the population doesn't think when they decide to make children. You, though, have lived through watching children die and families dissolve. You have also spent your life delivering both good and bad news about children. So, you think way too much everyday about this sort of thing to live it in your personal life."

Morti wasn't wrong. Aiden knew he wasn't wrong, Tripp knew he wasn't wrong, hell, the hospice nurse knew he wasn't wrong.

"It still sucks, though."

"Yep, but don't get me wrong, I'm in the same boat as you. I couldn't stand to watch my own kid die. You have to think about these things. Especially now, bringing them into this climate, I mean come on, look at London, practically underwater half the time."

"Thanks for trying Morti but just let me wallow, okay?"

"Fine, but if you're going to wallow, can we trade magazines? I'm done with the Nature one."

Tripp threw his magazine over to Morti and paused for a minute.

Morti knows too much about me. He pinned all my issues into one paragraph. I watched my brother die, my family dissolve, and then I spent the rest of my life trying to put families together. Now I'm here and I haven't built one for myself.

1 SEPTEMBER 2035

MOSCOW, RUSSIA

Slavomir was sitting in the dining room of his Moscow apartment with Anna. The children were playing in their bedroom.

"It's sad, the Tripp thing," Anna said. She wasn't wrong. It was sad.

"He is a good man. I'm thankful for him." Slavomir always appreciated what Tripp had done for him and Anna.

"If only we could return the favor."

"If only."

"Can you get me another coffee? I need to make a phone call," Slavomir asked, gesturing with his cup.

She took the cup and traced her hand up his arm. They loved each other fiercely, even more so after the children were born. *Thank you Dr. Tripp. Now let's make your job legal.*

He checked his watch, a nine hour time difference is annoying but the Senator should be up.

"Hello?"

"Senator, how are you?"

"It's midnight here Mr. Krukov, what do you want?"

"Oh I didn't realize you went to bed early. I wanted to call and tell you Dr. Tripp is dying."

"What? What does that mean? Hold on, hold on a second."

You could hear the rustling of the bed as the Senator got up to take the call elsewhere.

"Okay, start again, what the fuck do you mean he is dying?"

"I mean, he is dying. Pancreatic cancer."

"Shit. They haven't cured that yet."

"No, from what I have been told it is painful and difficult to cure."

"What does that have to do with me?"

"You are going to help us legalize the editing business so that way the team can remain in business."

"Why the hell would I do that? Who would be running the business anyways? That piece of shit was everything."

"Be careful Senator, you are talking about a dying man." He let that sink in for a moment.

"You met Dr. Tripp, but there are others who support the organization. There are others who can do what he can do. We have a transition plan, but you are part of it. To answer your question, you will be helping us legalize our business because if you do not, we will come to your ranch in Arkansas in the middle of the night and kill you, your wife, your two boys and your little girl, as promised."

"How do you want me to help you legalize this whole thing?"

"We are asking for our editing on embryos to be legalized for health purposes. Then, we can talk about cosmetic purposes later."

"That sounds like two favors to me."

"Good thing you have three children, Mr. Senator. Propose the bill, honor Dr. Tripp, and stop playing around. I'll watch the news."

Slavomir hung up the phone as Anna was bringing in his coffee. She kissed him.

"How did it go?"

"Good. I was arranging a present for Tripp."

"Who are you calling now?"

"Aiden."

"Where is he anyways?"

"Running an errand for me with Alex."

Slavomir put the phone to his ear.

"Everything is set, he'll do it." Slavomir didn't wait for a response. He hung up the phone and sipped his coffee.

XXXIV.

AS THE EARLY MORNING SUN TOUCHED UPON the hills of Woodland Cemetery, a trail of cars lined the path. The caravan snaked through the cemetery, ending just before the entrance. It was an interesting crowd. There were many families with healthy children, looking to pay respects to the man that made their dreams come true. Morti, Tara, Michelle, Aiden and Tony were all in attendance, all crying to some degree.

Looking out over the funeral, Slavomir, Anna and their two children stood on a grassy knoll, flanked by Alex and Arkady. Slavomir watched the priest gesture while the crowd bowed their heads, children fidgeting through the process. Slavomir tried to make out the faces. He recognized a few but not nearly as many as he thought he would.

Scooping up Leo, Slavomir pointed to the coffin. "Do you see that brown box over there?" The little boy nodded his head, squinting to see. "That is called a coffin."

The boy had never heard the word before. He found it very odd that they were standing away from everyone else. "What's a coffin?" Leo asked.

Slavomir smirked. "It's a home for dead people."

"Gross!" the little boy decried. Slavomir laughed. It was a little gross if you thought about it. Why do we put our dead in really nice boxes?

"In that box is a very good friend of mine. He helped me become your father," Slavomir told the boy. He wasn't lying. Slavomir had considered Tripp a friend. Tripp had never failed him.

"I like him," Leo said. He loved his dad and anyone who made that happen was a good person, according to the young boy.

"I do too," Slavomir said with some finality. He bounced Leo in his arms, sending the boy's hair back and forth in the air.

In that moment, Morti stepped up to deliver the eulogy. Dressed in a black suit and overcoat, he took a second to compose himself. This was tough for Morti, saying goodbye to his dear friend.

"I'd like to thank you all for coming today. Dr. Allen Galloway, or Tripp as we all called him, was a remarkable man. He dedicated his life to helping others build families and making the impossible possible. I'm proud to call him a colleague and a friend. Don't get me wrong, he drove me crazy. He was so high on caffeine that he couldn't stop bouncing his leg. He was constantly late and never wanted to work on holidays. Overall, a real lazy partner."

The group chuckled. Morti paused. He was getting choked up. As he tried to regain composure, he looked up. Out in the distance, he saw the tall Russian and his family, watching from the hill.

"But I wouldn't have traded him for the world. As we look around today, we see the fruits of his labor. He has cured so many people and rid the world of so much pain. I thank him for that and I'm going to miss him."

Morti looked up again, this time locking eyes with Slavomir. They held each other's gaze for a brief moment. Holding Leo in his arms, Slavomir turned around and disappeared from the hill.

EPILOGUE

THE COUPLE WAS EAGER FOR THEIR APPOINT-
ment as they traipsed through Manhattan. As they zigged and zagged across town, they kept thinking about their future child. They had been thinking about a girl. They wanted a tall girl, hopefully smart and athletic. Maybe she could be a doctor? They always fell back on, as long as she is healthy, we will be happy. That was always the line for normal, not astronomically wealthy, parents. As normal people, a teacher and sales associate, dreaming about a superstar child was out of the question. The initial packages provided by GS Editing were fifty-thousand dollars. No one had fifty-thousand dollars just lying around. The reasons they gave for the incredibly high price made sense.

"Science is expensive."

"Safety is our top priority for your child."

The real reason was probably that people would pay top dollar to make sure their child had the best chance in life. Look at Harvard, Yale and Brown. They are expensive. They churn out ambassadors and presidents. This will be the same thing for GS Editing. In fact, their track record so far shows the oldest children performing above average by a significant amount.

Now, though, this urbane couple from Rhode Island could dream. They couldn't believe their luck. They had been granted a Galloway Genomic Grant, or the Triple G, as the world called it.

The application was intense. They need letters of recommendation, two interviews, full body screens and a parenting essay. GS Editing reported that they received fifty million applications last year alone. That's fifty million applications for ten grants.

The light changed and the couple crossed the street to a glass building in Chelsea. They presented themselves to the armed guards standing outside. Once admitted, it led them to an outdoor atrium, lined with more armed guards and a pretty fountain. At the end of the atrium was an escalator. This escalator took them up to the waiting room. After checking in, they looked around the opulent waiting room. It felt like a spaceship.

When their names were called by a friendly nurse, she gave them a full tour of the facility. They saw the custom labor and delivery ward, the recovery areas and the editing labs. Everything looked clean and modern. Finally, they were escorted to a conference room that had a glass table. There was a full bar and coffee station along the back wall. They sat, being barely able to control themselves.

Approximately fifteen minutes later, a shorter man walked in and introduced himself. He was one of the consulting physicians on staff for GS Editing. He congratulated them on winning the Triple G and jumped into the consultation.

"This will take approximately three hours. You don't have any commitments after this, do you?" he asked politely. It could have taken thirty-six hours, the couple wasn't going anywhere. You cleared your calendar if you were lucky enough to be awarded a Triple G.

"Great, let me bring up the materials you will need." He tapped on the glass table and a series of documents appeared.

"These documents represent our privacy policies, the stipulations you agree to if you accept the Triple G and what the Triple G includes. We have provided these to you in advance, do you have any questions or concerns?"

The couple read them briefly. They knew that their child would be studied closely for the rest of their lives. They also knew that they got free health care. The couple was thinking of moving to New York just to access that free health care. They would not be able to access it in Rhode Island. GS Editing did not have an office there. It was actually becoming a trend for the parents to move to GS Editing office locations in order to keep that healthcare for life. They even took care of the parents! For the United States, that meant that there were populations mostly in New York, Los Angeles, Denver and Miami. Ethicists and Geneticists alike are concerned as this might throw off the population genetics. Specifically, they are concerned about the potential for speciation. If speciation did occur, this would mean that the GS edited children were different enough from normal humans that they would be considered a different species altogether. It would be like Gorillas and Humans, except in this case it would be Humans and Edited Humans.

Once again, the couple couldn't care less. They would let the professionals and the government handle those types of problems. The good news was that the government did not appear concerned.

They signed everything immediately through the micro blood sampler embedded in the glass table.

This led to an overview of all of the potential options that could be chosen. The list was extensive but could be broken down into approximately seven categories.

I. Sex

II. Physical Appearance

III. Overall Health

IV. Cognitive Abilities

V. Ancestry-derived Traits

VI. Athletic Abilities

VII. Extraneous Traits

As they made their way through the list of traits, they would often fall prey to the "elite" level add-ons. Those were not included in the Triple G but you could pay for them. The Triple G covered all basic level editing packages, any cosmetic work and one elite package. The most commonly chosen was the intellectual package. Everyone wanted their child to be smart and attractive. They watched their child grow before their eyes on the table, as did the price. When they were completed, they made tweaks here and there. She looked too good to be true.

"So, she looks absolutely wonderful," the doctor said. "When we account for the Triple G, the price comes out to approximately twenty-five thousand, four-hundred and eighty-seven dollars, plus tax."

The couple was shocked. They couldn't afford that.

"Now if you can't pay upfront, we do have payment plans. You could also go back and remove the extras, which would bring the cost down. It's completely up to you."

The doctor gave them a minute to discuss their options. When he returned, he helped them navigate removing two extras, and then working out a payment plan. They removed the enhanced spatial awareness gene set and the enhanced night vision genes. Their child will cost them approximately fifteen thousand dollars.

"Congratulations. I'll print out your paperwork and a picture of this rendering for you. Our finance team will come in to get everything set up for you."

The polite doctor shook their hands and left promptly. The couple was stunned. In a matter of three hours, they had created the perfect baby girl.

They started discussing names and chatted with the finance people. The finance people made the couple extremely aware that if they defaulted on their payment plan, there would be large consequences. The government had given them incredible leeway in this regard. They could take your house, if they deemed it necessary. It was almost better to get a loan from the bank, pay GS Editing and go bankrupt with the bank. With a quick finger prick, they signed the paperwork.

As they walked out and started their commute back to Rhode Island, they kept staring at the rendering of their beautiful baby.

She was perfect.